Copyright © 2023 I

Copyright © 2023 Izzy Coco Copyright © 2
Izzy Coco All rights reserved

The characters and events portrayed in this book are fictitious. Any similarity to real persons, living or dead, is coincidental and not intended by the author.

No part of this book may be reproduced, or stored in a retrieval system, or transmitted in any form or by any means, electronic, mechanical, photocopying, recording, or otherwise, without express written permission of the publisher.

Authored by: Izzy Coco - Human Authored
Cover design by: Izzy Coco

First Edition

CONTENTS

Copyright
Preface
Chapter 1 — 1
Chapter 2 — 7
Chapter 3 — 12
Chapter 4 — 25
Chapter 5 — 34
Chapter 6 — 42
Chapter 7 — 50
Chapter 8 — 72
Chapter 9 — 81
Chapter 10 — 85
Chapter 11 — 96
Chapter 12 — 119
Chapter 13 — 130
Chapter 14 — 137
Chapter 15 — 143
Chapter 16 — 156
Chapter 17 — 161
Chapter 18 — 170
Epilogue — 177

Smutastic Extra Epilogue: Jingle Bells, Jiggling All The Way	179
Thank you for reading.	185

PREFACE

Heads Up:-
While this is a romantic book, there are heavy erotic elements. The book is also written in British English with some informal language used.

AI Position:-
 AI has not been used for any aspect of this novel.

CHAPTER 1

Zasha

Hiring someone to pretend to be romantic with you is hardly a heartwarming way to spend Christmas, but sometimes needs must. Especially when the rest of your family are in Barbados, having barbeques on the beach, making merry to Soca– with crazy Aunty Bernice bothering the barmen with her loose hands.

No, while they do that, I will be spending what rare snatches of free time I have in London paying a strange man to utter sweet nothings in my ear. All to distract me from the fact that two weeks ago I was brutally dumped at Alton Towers just as my now ex-boyfriend Cornelius and I boarded a rollercoaster, leaving me both sobbing from a broken heart and terrified with vertigo.

According to Cornelius, our breakup is my punishment for being a workaholic, "Dating you is like getting intimate with a rubber band. While I know you're stretching to make things work, at some point you're going to snap just because you're not sleeping and you're existing off gummy bears."

When he told me that, my immediate worry went to what that boy had been doing to my stationery.

Anyway, it's not entirely fair. I work as a software engineer and sometimes when we get to the end of a project you have crunch time to deal with. During crunch time, the team toil like crazy to get a solution live. Unfortunately, we often have crunch time right before the holidays.

So here I stand, right in front of the Rent-A-Romance office for my initial consultation.

Take a deep breath girl, until you sign the dotted line you're not a sad sack...yet.

After Cornelius, I felt damned miserable. I stopped working long hours for a little while and decided to focus on getting some time to myself, maybe getting some real romance under my belt.

Instead, I accidentally stumbled upon Rent-A-Romance; a romantic role-play service. Needless to say, I was intrigued. According to their website, Rent-A-Romance offers a range of romantic scenarios to role-play based on your desired tropes. You would then be allocated a man called a 'Romancer.' This fellow would play the male protagonist opposite you; his lady love.

The testimonials were glowing, and when I looked across the web I only found effusive praise. A bit of romantic cheer this time of year was just what I needed. So, I booked in for a consultation.

However...once I have my first Rent-A-Romance session I'll be the girl who has to pay for my romantic encounters. I mean, what kind of person does that make me? I'm not even getting boned for my money.

Standing in front of the building, a neon sign greets with the name of the service "Rent-A-Romance!"

Sighing, I open the entrance door and step into the office's waiting room.

It looks just as seedy as I feel. The walls are adorned with posters of oiled men whose tanned abs are rocking serious eight-packs, because six is not enough. There are plastic pink chairs in the waiting room.

Two women are sitting in the waiting area which has the ambience of a local surgery; sombre, brown and smelling of anaesthetic. Both are wearing large hats and sunglasses, with their heads buried in magazines as if they couldn't hide themselves enough.

I find a chair with as much equidistance between them, regretting that I too am not wearing a decent disguise. Without one I feel exposed. Sinking into my chair I imagine the headlines...

Extra Extra! Nerd has to pay for romance; so says two women also paying for romance. Read all about it!

A beeping sound buzzes throwing me out of my errant reveries. This is followed by a gong and then a shout in a croaky American accent, "Come in!"

I potter on through.

The office has a peculiar, dated feel. There is a plastic palm tree in the corner near the door with a bit of ragged gold tinsel strangling it. Next to that is a bookcase filled with old books about accountancy and how to make your own website. The walls are a hue that can most flatteringly be described as stained yellow, accentuated by a mottled blue and grey carpet. It's the sort of place where souls go to die.

What is startling however is the man sat on the old oak desk right in the middle of the large room; with black leather sofas flanked on the left and right. It is hard to tell his real age. He looks supernaturally unhealthy, as if body parts have fallen off him and have had to be glued back on. If I had to hazard a guess, I would say he is seventy. But, he could be thirty, or he could be three hundred. He is hooked up to an oxygen tank gasping in air through a mask with one hand and fiddling for a cigarette in an open box with another. As if dicing with his own life is not satisfying enough – he wants the thrill of taking out anyone else in this room.

"Welcome beautiful, welcome. I'm Hamish. Come in. Sit down, sit. Sit!" he splutters phlegmatically and gestures to the chair opposite in a wild fashion.

You know those people you automatically feel tense around? You know the ones, they might be your serial killers, clowns or internal auditors. Some people just have that way about them. You want to escape their company by your claws. This man has that, but he is also the ticket to the closest thing I will ever taste to a romance for the ages.

"Thank you," I say primly, smoothing down my denim trousers and nervously bouffing my afro bun.

"So just wanna say thank you for completing the form Miss Williams. Boy oh boy have we got some tasty stories for you," Hamish licks his lips. I wince at this overfamiliar man.

He chuckles at my visible reaction, "So you wanna go pirate, dark romance, hockey romance and Christmas holiday for the first-month subscription? That gives you your four sessions."

"That would be nice, yes please," I meekly respond. Oh this is so mortifying; well, at least he's enjoying himself.

Hamish's saggy face arranges itself like loose elastic bands into a sinister expression that resembles a lecherous smile, "Oh ho ho lady! We're going to light up your lights this Christmas, oh yes we are sugar. You can bet on it!"

He finally lights up his cigarette with a chrome lighter shaped like a naked lady's torso.

The cigarette lights up, the room doesn't explode. I breathe a little easier, in part because I hope removing oxygen from the room through my respiration will lessen the likelihood of becoming part of an impromptu firework display.

Then he leans in and splutters while coughing, "So sweet lips-" being called that does something funny to my face.

"-What'll it be? A taste of the vanilla, chocolate or another pudding?" yuck. I mean, why? Hamish gasps in air using the mask attached to his oxygen tank before setting that aside and taking a hearty drag of his cigarette.

Timidly I shuffle in my chair, "I don't mind on ethnicity. A nice man will do, someone convincing who doesn't treat me like a pity case."

"What about the body? You like 'em buff, like 'em lean? Short king, mountain man? What you want?"

"Someone who can act as if they really do like me. I would appreciate that," nudging my glasses back I nervously wonder what kind of men they have on their books. The website didn't have any profiles of the Romancers.

I don't ask for much, I don't think. I mean, if they're a god-awesome hunk that would help.

"Great – we'll match someone up with you! Now just to give you the format. Over the next four Sundays we have some studios here with the best atmosphere! The best theatrics! The only exception is hockey romance, for that you need to go to an ice rink. We recommend Village Green Ice Stadium, they don't freak out at our pretend hockey players."

I pull a face, "An actual ice rink? That's a bit embarrassing. I can't skate, will *he* be able to?"

Hamish shrugs, "It works, you'll see. All my men can skate like champs."

Cigarette ash drops onto the floor but he doesn't care. Hamish splutters more and then places the oxygen mask on his face, gasping painfully. That oxygen tank is making me nervous, as is Hamish. I cannot wait to get out.

"So scripts, props, everything, we'll ship 'em to you. Just meet your date, or Romancer if you will, at the venue from nine-thirty in the morning, you get 'em for the whole day."

I'm about to ask about nights. However Hamish sees the eager twinkle in my eye and so he waves his finger, "Na-uh-uh. No hanky panky. You can smooch but no tongue. Your Rent-A-Romance man will be keeping his trouser snake in his burrow. We're dealing with professionals here."

Yeesh.

"Okay, sounds good," I squeak softly, pushing up my glasses with a finger again. It's a nervous reflex and this is not a comfortable discussion.

As I walk out of Rent-A-Romance I see a woman emerge with ten hunky men of different ethnicities dressed in regency outfits. Wow, so many Romancers. Rent-A-Romance must have a lot of them on its books if they can use ten for a single session.

CHAPTER 2

Jai

I need to move out of the flat I share with my ex-girlfriend. Last night I went into the fridge and saw she had placed post-it notes of our names 'Jai' and 'Nellie' on every single food item.

The only problem is that I'm still in my probation period at work, so I can't exactly ask if they'd spare me an instant pay rise so I can scarper.

Nellie and I broke up a month ago but we stupidly moved into a house we bought together six months back, even though I already had a hunch that she was trouble. Her behaviour got a lot worse when we moved in together. She would cut holes in my clothes when I was out of the house; and when I asked her about it she would blame the moths. These moths must have been the size of bats.

Then there was the time I found a hidden camera in a very suspect teddy bear that Nellie had planted on top of the drawers opposite our bed. The giveaway was its flashing red eyes.

But weirdly I was able to justify her growing craziness towards me, when you're in that situation you normalise it. It was when she turned it on other people that I decided enough was enough.

The last straw was when we went shopping and she pushed two old ladies on Zimmer frames out of the way at TK MAXX; sending them sprawling on the floor, just to get at the last of a designer glittery knit vest.

So I broke things off. At first there was rage; she set fire to my shoes and cut up my passport. But then eerie calm; like she was in some form of denial. It doesn't feel comfortable. I lock my bedroom door when I am sleeping, you know, just in case she's feeling unexpectedly stabby one day. It must be what it's like to be trapped in a cage with gorillas, they'll be nice to you for a bit – maybe even offer you one of their hair fleas as a snack. You might even think they're your friends, until they rip your arms off and gobble up your face.

So here we are. I'm lumbered with a joint mortgage with a monster ex who thinks that when people call her a 'sociopath' it means she gives out extra nice hugs.

Somehow, until I sort something out with Nellie, I need to keep paying my bit of the mortgage, and eventually rent a place of my own. Here in London. Where these days if an old lady wanted to live in a shoe, she'd be priced out of the rental market by fifty other people who wouldn't mind the thought of living in a pungent leather abode. Anything to be close to Buckingham Palace.

These are the thoughts that trouble me as I walk through the streets trying to find a place to eat my coronation chicken sandwich during my lunch break.

I'm a gangly chap, who can see over most people's heads. So even in crowded London it's not hard to spot a spare park bench placed inside a very sweet little park. Pleased with my find I go and sit down on the bench and tuck into my delicious sandwich. However, it's facing what looks like a proper skeevy business called 'Rent-A-Romance.' Wonder what they do there. Probably prostitution.

As I ponder this, an elderly man brandishing a small gas tank under his arm comes running out of the dubious establishment that I am warily staring at.

His eyes are determinedly trained on a burly brute of a man who is walking the street in front of the park where I am now sat. The guy has so much thigh muscle that the pedestrian pavement practically quakes under his every step.

The elderly dude with the oxygen tank hobbles up and cries out, "Hey you, handsome! Come here! Have I got a proposition for you!"

The man who he is pointing to runs off as fast as his beefy legs will carry him. Instead, I'm left looking at Mr Oxygen Tank. He screws his face up in disappointment, "Aww fuck! Was going for the hench fella, but guess you'll to do."

I shake my head, "Naw mate. You're alright," I wave him off with my hand.

"What, you don't like the idea of spending your Sundays being someone's fantasy? Two thousand pounds a month for a few cuddles. What do you say?" says Mr Oxygen Tank, licking his lips at me.

What a dirty old fella.

"Naw, not my thing mate. Chin up though bruv, I'm sure you'll find a man who will help you with your…your…you know."

Mr Oxygen Tank cackles in a low sinister fashion. Glad it's not nighttime in the park – this man has the vibe of a wrong one; the sort of person that television streaming services dream of to supply their true crime offerings.

"No you knucklehead, I *love* women, like *luuurve* them. Love them. So much so that I have a special service for the little ladies, called Rent-A-Romance. The *señoritas* can book out romantic encounters of their…predilections…fantasies and just indulge a little," Mr Oxygen Tank stalks towards me.

I take another bite out of my sandwich. The situation is up to the nines in fishy, "Let me guess. You want me to tart myself out to one of these women. If you're a legit fella, tell us, why are you dragging strangers out of parks to pimp them out to your ladies?

Won't the women have something to say about that if they're paying in the thousands?"

"I'm desperate, used up all my performers for a reverse harem story; the girl paid an extra fee for all ten of my guys. And we need the money, any chump change helps for the holidays. You know the deal," he sits next to me and spreads his legs as wide as a man possibly can. Edging away I keep nibbling on my sandwich gingerly.

Mr Oxygen Tank then continues, "And it's not 'tarting out.' It's a very respectful, classy wooing of the ladies. You just need to whetten their appetite if you catch my drift. But keep your flute squeaky clean. Running for mayor next year and I need to maintain a reputable operation."

Chortling at the notion of this guy having the puppet strings over the lives of those living in my city, I nearly choke on my sandwich. Spluttering away I beat my fist to my chest to cough up the offending crumbs.

"You, for mayor?!" I laugh – until I remember the current state of Western democracy and realise that this man could have Britain on a stick. At this thought, I chew my sandwich sombrely.

Mr Oxygen Tank grins, "Yeah me for mayor. What you saying? Look. You'll get paid some real green just to get a girl to cream her pants. What's not to love? Two thousand I tell ya. What you workin' as now?"

I shouldn't tell this man anything but fuck it – it's a real-life experience to talk to someone this terrible, "Video game designer."

Mr Oxygen Tank retorts, "Pfft! What the fuck ever is that? VHS designs itself."

VHS? Debating the merits of my chosen career may be futile here, so I shrug.

He keeps going, "Designing VHS games. That ain't the money. That ain't the money. If you do this, maybe you can pay some real bills. It will be great to finally have a Mexican round here anyways."

I cringe at his blunder, "I'm half Malay, half Welsh."

"What the fuck!? Where are the tropes in that?! Nah you're not. Get out of town! What the fuck is a Welsh? What the fuck is a Malay?! Get outta here!"

With Mr Oxygen Tank shaking his oxygen tank at me with racist ire for not being tropey enough, I start to see red.

This is bang out of order. I'm not going to have this dickhead talking to me this way, "Fuck right off will you? Don't know what you're playing at but this is rubbish. You're a bigot. Fuck off alright?"

"Easy, easy, calm down!" he's talking to me as if I'm an irascible horse that is threatening to canter off.

"Look, try a session out – this Sunday, you'll get sweet money for it. Bet you could do with the money. Everyone in London could do with the money," like the bloody devil he speaks in honeyed tones.

It's true.

Fuck it. Defeated by poverty and desire to escape Nellie's clutches my pride ebbs away into the fiery pits of destitution, "Alright, where do I sign up?"

CHAPTER 3

Zasha

~Pirate Romance – A Bodice Ripper~

So, it turns out that putting down the equivalent of two months of salary for an out-of-this-world romance experience buys you a pink ball gown costume that looks like it escaped from a cake shop. There are bows of every colour adorning the voluminous fabric, and it has a bustline so low that you can nearly see my belly button. This came in a packet labelled 'Pirate Experience.' I tipped the packet upside down to see if anything else was enclosed such as something to obscure all that cleavage showing and nope, it's just this tasteful number.

It was only when I was stood outside a studio door ominously numbered sixty-nine -no doubt by the genius that is Hamish- that it occurred to me; I could have worn *something else* – not just the fever dream of a dirty old man who likes frills and bosom spills.

Anyway, here I am, I've done my hair in a Regency-style updo and added a little rouge to my cheek and lips. Dangly pearl earrings drip from my ears as if this will help salve my gaudy appearance. I mean, because you know, more is more.

Putting in my contact lenses while peering in my bathroom mirror; my nerves got the better of me making the outfit cling to me with anxious sweat. This wasn't helped by navigating the tube with an extra poufy dress. Nothing could hide the noisy outfit under my coat as I travelled to Dalston where the Rent-A-Romance studios are based, and I did get some curious glances on the underground. To make matters worse it is a super-hot day, and I am sweating like a fountain in Piccadilly Circus. My face is flushed. I am hoping my nose is not sweating. I always get a sweaty nose.

What I am wearing now is a massive departure from how I usually dress; I like to think of it as loose dark academia chic, however my mum calls my style frumpcore. I am probably overly conscious of my body, the wobbly bumpy bits that no gym will tame, no diet will erase. But it doesn't matter because this man is getting paid to flatter me. He *has* to at least pretend to like how I look.

My 'date' is late. Ten minutes…he is eating into my time. I take out my phone and start tapping an email to Hamish. I am feeling nervous as it is, my hands are sweaty and the dress is like a blinking sauna. It must be all that natural material it's made of, not.

However I then hear a cough and then a gravelly, low greeting, "Hello Zasha."

Turning around I see a tall, lean guy with broad shoulders and an attractive countenance. He stuns me. He has a pirate patch, pirate hat, a fake green parrot on his shoulder, a fake goatee beard that the Noughties want back, a plastic hook hand and a spiky silver codpiece at his groin. My gaze fixes on the spiky codpiece, now I've seen it I cannot unsee it. You could turn other people into one-eyed pirates with those spikes.

He coughs again, "Erm, eyes up here. Or eye, eye matey! Ha! Um."

It's with that I realise my gaze has been fixed in horror at his silver codpiece. I look stricken up into his one exposed eye, unartfully slathered as it is with kohl eyeliner.

My mouth moves wordlessly like a fish, oh I am mortified, "Oh ah. Right, shall we?"

Curtsying and bowing at the same time I do a weird royal wave thing with my hand to beckon him to the door. What on earth am I doing? The shiny reflection from his silver codpiece must have fried my brain.

He says nothing as he opens the door, grimacing as if he were embarrassed for me. I'm embarrassed for me.

Following him in through the door I trip on the many layers of my gown with an *oomph!* My house keys spill out, my phone goes clattering on the floor. I land flat on my face, right by his lavish pirate boots.

My 'date' gasps uttering 'Fuck! Urgh uh – fire in the hole! Here, let's help you up."

Offering his hand he tries to grasp mine but I still cannot get my footing now that I have been felled. My feet are entangled by the billowing fabric of my dress. I hopelessly flop around like a beached drunk.

In the end he says, "Here" and scoops me in his arms before staggering through the door. I look into his one exposed eye and think how gorgeous it is under the makeup, almost feline. The thought gives me a tingle in the belly, and I smile and sigh in satisfaction. Not sure how Hamish did it, but he managed to snag a man for me who is rather…dashing. Perhaps it is just the pirate outfit that is having that effect. Hamish may seem like an old goat, and yet he has the matchmaking instincts of a seasoned Dobble player.

"What's your name?" I ask as he gazes at me with particular intensity.

His singular eye grazes the length of my body, "Jai. But that's Pirate Captain Jai 'Longsilver'" Maddox to you."

He smiles and his grip relaxes. Unfortunately, this results in him lowering his hold and as a result, my bottom makes contact with his spiked codpiece.

"OWW!" Arching my back as a natural reflex to break free, I

inadvertently end up headbutting Jai in the jaw.

Jai yells in pain, "Son of a bi-biscuit!" he huffs as he staggers into the studio. His plastic hook hangs off his hand while his trusty toy parrot flops over as if it were pecking his armpit.

His grip loosens from the surprise of the blunt force and as a result I plop unceremoniously on the floor, bouncing on my bottom but otherwise fine. Ever since Jai arrived I feel I've had more falls than Niagara. We haven't even known each other ten minutes.

"Oh I am so sorr- I mean uh, shiver me timbers, uh. Sorry," he says as he rubs his jaw with the curve of his hook. His fake goatee has now lost its position, bestowing him with a startled, askew appearance.

He offers his hand to me and pulls me up.

Finally arising I feel flustered and extra hot, my forehead coated in beads of sweat.

"Need to take my coat off, it's hot in here," I mutter. I wonder if my dress has sweat patches, this thought makes me feel even hotter with the thought of impending embarrassment.

I unzip my coat quickly to cool down. It's not a real date but I don't want to be remembered by Jai as the sweatiest sweat monster he's ever been paid to have a romance with.

"Oh wow," I hear Jai utter at my obscenity of a dress, and if things couldn't get worse gravity has been unkind and both my nipples are nearly showing. There is a sharp intake of air from him – undoubtedly disapproval- as I try and drag up the dress and salvage my pride. There is very little to salvage.

His codpiece suddenly pops off, unveiling a crotch stuffed so tightly with socks that his trousers are threatening to split.

By now I feel ridiculously hot, embarrassed, ashamed. I start flapping my hands trying to cool down, blowing air up to my face by jutting out my lower lip as I huff. My cheeks are burning like a cosy hearth. My only recourse is to take the dress off, but I can't do that, I have nothing else to wear. Just a very ugly pair of orange underpants that I have had too long in my possession since university and a mismatching green bra I stole from my sister.

"Oh my god I feel faint, so faint. I can't breathe in enough air," I feel dizzy and light on my feet, as if I am on a ship, which is appropriate as we are standing next to the type of wooden pirate ship you get in a playground. Glancing around I notice that the room – the size of a tennis court- is painted a colour that can best be described as abandoned swimming pool blue, with an inflatable shark idly in the middle of the room.

I steady myself on the little pirate ship.

Suddenly, overcome with giddiness I keel over, but Jai catches me in his arms.

Desperately gulping in air, I cannot help but note that Jai looks worried, "Zasha! Zasha! Stay with me!"

He frantically unpeels his pirate patch to get a better view, revealing one eye that is nude of makeup. To free me of my offending constraining clothing Jai attempts to scrape off my dress using both his normal hand and his plastic hook hand. However, because of my sweaty skin the dress stubbornly clings on. Jai swears like the filthiest of sea scallywags and using his two hands, rips open the bodice of my dress tearing it apart with a rip roar louder than thunder on the high seas. Thus, all is revealed; my bumpy bits, my mismatching lingerie, my sweaty self.

Me.

Death at the hands of a pirate wouldn't be the worst thing in the world right now.

What a travesty.

Closing my eyes, I pretend that perhaps if I can't see him, then maybe he can't see me, and this is all just an overpriced nightmare.

Opening my eyes I see Jai's maw – his mouth wide open- coming slowly down upon my own. He's trying to Moby Dick me. I freak the hell out.

"Hey Hannibal, save that for the Dark Romance session!" I blurt, scurrying to my feet. He scrambles up with me.

"That's not what I -" he protests.

Before he can respond I jab his chest with my finger, "What kind of kiss was that?!"

"The kiss of life! You passed out," he places his hook hand against his chest as if he's swearing from his heart. Jai gazes at me with the deepest sincerity. By now his fake goatee is hanging off a cheek and his parrot is gently bungee jumping off his shoulder. His eyes travel from my face to my neck to my exposed body. There is a devious quirk of his lips. He cannot possibly be perving however, not at this misshapen nerd. Nah. It's probably mirth, that a girl like me is so desperate for romance I would pay to be doing this on my free Sunday, it's pathetic.

I've had enough.

I sigh, "Let's just call it quits. This really isn't working out, is it?"

He walks towards me slowly, like a big cat attempting to capture a snack. To maintain a distance I walk slowly back until I am pressed against the pirate ship. As he prowls in my direction he drawls, "If it's a better kiss you want, shall we try again? What about something like…"

He looks down into my eyes, his gaze dancing with what small glints of light the overhanging lightbulb affords.

He cups my chin between his thumb and forefinger and runs a finger down the side of my jaw. Shivering from the feathery sensation, I gaze at him, yearning for his attention.

Jai's lips brush against mine, arching my back hungrily I try to capture them into a kiss. He draws back teasingly, his eyes glinting with mischief.

"Nah uh, patience Zasha," I feel his thumb brush against my lower lip, and he groans, the socks in his underpants pushing up against me.

"God you're fucking sexy," he growls. I whimper instinctively as a honeyed sensation curls within my belly. This is good; I'll have to throw an extra something in Hamish's coffers for the drawn out teasing, the dialogue. Bravo.

"You've already ripped my bodice Captain Jai Longsilver, what else will you pillage next?" I exclaim, having a bit of fun getting into character, trying to diffuse the crackle of tension in the air. He's a professional, he'll flow with it.

Except he looks at me, like a man unleashed and I feel him grab under my knee and wrap my leg around his waist, his breath caressing my hot cheeks. Then his hand grasps my bottom *tight*. Possessively. Certainly beyond health and safety levels of grasping. I inhale sharply looking into his dark eyes, drowning in them a little. I can't look away. Neither can he it seems.

And he swoops in, his tongue forcing its way between my lips; a shock of arousal zips through my body and drenches me within my core. Jai's nose brushes against my own and he groans as his tongue caresses my own.

Wow, tongues - isn't that a Hamish no-no?

Jai

Well, I'm sporting a rager. It pinged my codpiece right off. Not surprised with Zasha *'but I'm just a shy sex vixen'* Williams. She doesn't seem to mind my erection pressed against her as I do a rubbish job of trying to keep it professional. She is all blushes and yet her flirting is outrageous, *"You've already ripped my bodice Captain Jai Longsilver, what else will you pillage next?"* She said breathlessly, her cleavage exposed and barely covered by a little bra, her panties showing a delicious camel toe. I had half a mind rip off the rest of that tattered dress and bury myself into her as she cried out my name in her sweet voice.

So yeah, I'm partial to her.

Oh who am I kidding, I want her pinned underneath, sobbing out my name.

Going full plundering pirate I kiss Zasha fiercely, my tongue possessively pressing between her inviting lips as her warm mouth takes me in, her tongue caressing against my own. When we kiss an electricity passes between us and encompasses my every part. Pressing my hardness against her luscious, curvy body, I have no idea what my end game is, all I know is that I've lost complete sense of civil behaviour around this sexy girl.

Moulding myself against Zasha, I squeeze her bottom in my hand, dragging her closer still. Her breathing hitches and she gazes deeply into me, her eyes half-lidded with lust. I'm behaving like a hungry raptor, but she isn't saying no, she is inviting it, welcoming it, kissing back. Zasha wraps her arms around my neck, her fingers idly stroking the nape. Zasha's tongue brushes against mine, furtively exploring as my lips caress against hers, persisting in letting her know what I want, that what I want is to drown in her.

Fuckkk...

I am not going to be able to take much more of this.

Just as I contemplate tearing off her little orange knickers with my teeth she delicately utters, "How much will this cost, this kiss with tongues? Is it an add-on? I mean, I know we can't *do it*. Hamish made that abundantly clear...."

My lust-addled mind is confused for a minute, until it occurs to me that she doesn't realise how turned on I am. She thinks *I am paid* to do this. My head spins, drunk from lust. If I tell her that it's all me, she might hightail if all she's looking for is a little bit of organised fun courtesy of Rent-A-Romance. However, if I play along….

"It's all included," I mutter. The tentacles of guilt tickle my conscious, yet with my blood having left my brain and made its home in my hardness I am desperate for this to continue. Desperate for her touch. I am a rubbish, horny human being.

Zasha presses her body against me, "Everything is included? *Everything*?"

"Oh yup, all is inclusive, everything that you want," I gruffly inform her with the enthusiasm of an overly accommodating holiday rep, my hand still cupping her bottom while drinking in her curves, hearing her breathing grow heavier every time I caress her. Zasha is trembling against me, further fraying at what little control I now possess.

"Uh, you know Hamish – doesn't like the extra services we offer to be spoken about, especially given that he is running for mayor, so we're best off keeping it quiet."

Truly I'm a dirty dog, it's official. There is probably a lonesome circle in hell, just for me. I try to shove the guilt further down, but I cannot ignore its glint.

With Zasha's back now firmly against the little pirate ship, she draws me in and I cannot resist kissing her, everything about her demands my attention. The tips of my fingers caress the soft dark skin of her wrists.

"A tempting delight aren't you, captive wench Zasha?" I taunt. Then taking in her lower lip, I gently bite it and Zasha releases the sweetest cry.

"Oh my god," she whimpers, her chin lifting up to meet my kiss, the soft curve of her jaw illuminated by the harsh overhanging light. Good - Zasha is enjoying this; just the thought of her arousal edges my own.

Clearing my throat, I attempt lamely to get back into character by whispering in her ear with as much severity as I can muster, "Get ready to be plundered Zasha."

My lips touch her earlobes and then I use the tip of my tongue to gently trace the shell of her ear, leaving a silvery trail.

"Tell me how much you want me pretty wench?" barely able to speak, my words are half-moaned.

"I want you Jai, Captain Jai," she says quietly.

"More," I have a bit of a dickish side, so I'm probably getting off on this a bit too much. But I love the sound of her voice. I bet even in the dark without touching, just hearing her speak would be a turn-on.

"God you're a fucking tease," Zasha moans, lightly quivering in anticipation of what is to come.

How can I resist her? Our gaze fuse together; as if tethered by a golden rope, drawing us in. The girl is a magnet, because I cannot stop wanting to kiss those lips, kiss *her*. Dipping my face so near to her own that our noses nearly touch, her feathery warm breath caresses my skin. She looks up at me, a profound expression etched upon her features, her deep brown eyes glistening like diamonds, alive with the promise of what is coming next.

I want to hear her moan around me.

With aching slowness my lips approach hers for a kiss. There is a sweet electricity that gently fizzes between us as our mouths murmur together, as if speaking a language of longing, before I can hold back no longer and I capture her mouth. My tongue, parts her lips greedily yearning for more, as she rocks against me, goading me to explore her. I inhale, committing her scent to my memory; sandalwood, vanilla…and another scent I cannot put my finger on, perhaps just her. My tongue finds her own and flickers lazily against it, like a pearl. Together our tongues dance and our lips find a rhythm that grows more needy as we both become undone.

She moans, a low vibration that emanates within my deepest most primal self. I am losing my head. But that's not what I am here for.

Breaking the kiss I run my fingers through my hair and try to gather my thoughts. Breathlessly I try to salvage the role play that we are performing, "Just so you understand delicious wench, this is my ship..." I gesture at the play ship which is slightly smaller than my height,"...and my rules on these here high seas. Understand lass?" I attempt to growl with pirate authenticity.

Zasha looks like she is snapping out of a dream, before she reorientates herself and presses against me enthusiastically, "I hope you're not going to take me, in the carnal sense, on this behemoth vessel."

"I absolutely am," purring deeply I trail my lips across her cheekbone. Zasha gasps dramatically, placing the back of her hand to her forehead as if she is truly giddy with the thought of being ravished. Well her nipples are as hard as little bullets, they're straining against her bra. Smiling devilishly, I scoop her into my arms, causing her to squeal from surprise and appetisingly cling to my neck. I step into the ship, which is easy to do, as it's tiny.

But as I am about to do bad things to her, the virtuous part of me whispers, *keep it in your pants Jai. Shagging her within fifteen minutes of our first meeting is not romantic.* Then that good part of me splutters, heaves its oxygen tank and goes out for a cigarette. For fuck's sake, how can my guardian angel be Hamish? Says it all about me really.

Sighing I decide to heed Hamish's advice and keep the action 'closed door.' Which means no smut at all. This is the only type of sex that's supposed to happen at Rent-A-Romance. The animal man within me is just going to have to hobble home with blue balls.

Placing Zasha back down on her feet I then loudly exclaim, "And then we get up to a whole manner of vices that no lady would ever feel comfortable declaring in polite company."

Zasha who had been looking forward to a dally on my mast gazes back wide-eyed. Her brows crash together like furious waves as if she has just spotted Satan, "Did you just, make that a *closed-door* scene?" she skulks towards me in the manner of an assassin, her back hunched, her fingers resembling claws. Her eyes pin me down as if I've curve-balled her the mother of all insults.

"Is that what you meant by sex, is that what all our encounters will be like?" she approaches even closer, nostrils flaring. She's pretty mad at me, I see this.

Chuckling at this angry, horny lady I capture her hands with mine, caressing her palms with my thumbs, "No, I just want you to go away and have a think about whether you want to do this. There's no rush."

"I only have three other sessions with you," Zasha bites her lower lip anxiously.

My lies pour forth, "We'll make up for it, we can have a catch-up session."

Her big brown eyes fixate upon my own, her lips tug into a slight smile at this promise. A sensation of sunshine courses from between my rib cage to my thoroughly frustrated hardness.

She is so pretty, beautiful really, but it's like she doesn't even know it. I inhale sharply as my heart beats faster just from looking at her. There is an intensity to her presence that makes it difficult to breathe.

Breaking my gaze before I do something stupid such as pin her underneath me like an overfamiliar luchador, I clear my throat.

I pull out the threadbare script Hamish provides us with should we struggle to improvise, "Right, let's see what Hamish has written here. Do you have your script? Hamish would have sent it with the dress." Zasha shakes her head, still looking mildly cheated of her opportunity at a jolly rogering.

Great, so I'm the only one with a script, but it's only a couple of pages. Maybe some of it is missing. We have like, over five hours to kill. Five awkward hours of her looking thoroughly vexed.

Fuck the pirate ship.

"Let's get out of here," I stuff the script into my pocket.

"Where will we go? What will I wear?" she looks down briefly at her provocatively torn outfit.

Hamish told me there are spare outfits for the performers in the little office located on site, "I'll find something."

CHAPTER 4

Zasha

He found me another pirate outfit, also with a hook, codpiece, parrot and eyepatch.

We look at each other bemused. Snap – we're porny-looking pirates.

God Jai's such a hottie, but my head is now spinning with confusion, and serious frustration. One can only ponder, is it scientifically possible to explode if you get too aroused without an avenue of *ahem*, release? Closed door sex scenes should be considered a crime, a high crime to expectant nether regions everywhere. I can't believe he did that to me after that delicious kiss and telling me with honeyed words how I could have everything ever from the sex menu. He meant everything ever in my imagination. I should abandon ship, but he is so sexy and compelling I cannot help but tag along.

We take the underground tube train to St Katharine Docks; and find seats next to each other. A disturbed person sitting opposite us exclaims, "Bloody pirates! I see you…oi! What did you do to the Mary Celeste? Fucking sea urchins."

We ignore him, avoiding eye contact as fastidiously as possible. If I was by myself, I would do what everyone else in London does when they're on the tube with society's more interesting elements and pretend to scroll my phone.

Jai leans forward and holding his hands together turns his head to the side to stare keenly at me, his brown hair cascading over his eyes, "So Zasha Williams, tell me about you? What does a girl like you do in the world?"

"That's a broad question, I could ask the same of you," I look at Jai like he's a giant ice cream and it's a hot summer's day. I am rocking some serious horn for this guy.

Jai chuckles to himself, "Okay, well let's start with a small talk classic. What do you do for fun?"

Tilting my head at Jai my lips curve into a wry saucy smile, "Nerd stuff. What about you?" I purposefully avoid the details. Some men get excited when I talk about my interests. Others run a mile. Even though this is a fake date, I don't want to bore Jai. It would be best to remain mysterious.

Jai stares at me even more keenly, "Snap. Also nerd stuff. I'm a video game designer; but I love games. That's what made me foolish enough to make it my day job."

This peaks my interest, "Oh yeah, what kind? I'm an RPG girl myself, and strategic. Skyrim baby."

I clap triumphantly, like I've just sunk hundreds of pounds in a casino game and won, when in reality I've sunk hundreds of hours in a video game with only a middling command of imaginary spells to show for it.

"Skyrim, what? Yeah, it's still brilliant, but why not Starfield – it's fucking awesome, have you not bothered with that yet?"

Shaking my head I sigh, "It doesn't have all the mods yet."

He cocks an eyebrow and looks at me super cheekily.

A flush creeps up my neck, "Geezus you perv, not those kind of mods!"

I whack his knee -because you know any excuse for physical contact, even the brutal variety- and he leans back, still smiling, as are his eyes. He places one hand where I whacked his knee and rubs it with his thumb. He's thinking I am keeping my game of Skyrim fresh with porny sex mods. Gross. But also completely accurate. I mean, come on, Argis the Bulwark isn't going to sheath his own sword.

His knee twitches and he is still fixing his gaze at me, I shuffle uncomfortably before Jai clears his throat, "So what do you do for work Zasha?"

He likes saying my name a lot, in a fashion that makes me feel entirely uncomfortable between the thighs, "I uh, I uh. I'm a software engineer, for a fintech product. It's dead exciting stuff, if you like your derivatives with a slice of functional programming."

Game development must be so thrilling. Trying to imagine it, I envisage that it would be a lot of glamour and the beautiful people of the software development world partying away and bonking all of the time while they worked.

"Game development is shit. The crunching is brutal, the pay mediocre. You work eighty hour weeks every day for three weeks with a bunch of other sleep deprived cranks, and then you get spat out crying at the end of your soul-crushing career," Jai pauses and taps his chin thoughtfully, "I love it, as a sadomasochist, it's brilliant."

"A-a- sado, sado…." it's impossible to string words together, just imagining Jai the dungeon master…or minion?

Jai's grin contorts to something more wolfish, "Your mind is whirring."

He leans in closer, his pupils boring into my own, "Have I broken you Zasha?"

I can't tell if he's joking. What a scamp, most certainly a sadistic scamp. A glow emanates from my fuzzy regions.

Keeping quiet I don't respond. Instead I awkwardly twiddle my thumbs all the way to our destination, occasionally shooting him darting glances, only to find that he still gazing at me like he would happily eat me alive.

St Katharine Docks is a busy marina nestled next to the Tower of London, surrounded by restaurants, shops and bars. Jai takes me to a pirate themed pub called 'Redbeard's Skull and Cross Tavern.' It's fantastic. It looks just like a pirate enclave.

I look around wondrously, and the man behind the bar grins. He's dressed like a pirate too. He's a tall, handsome chap with dreadlocks.

"Aye aye fair lady, what can I get for ye today? I'd say we could serve ye up the catch of the day..." the barman says before leaning in, "...but that looks like you."

What a charmer the barman is, but I bet he's uttered that line a million times. Probably a great way to get some tips.

I look at Jai who appears slightly red-faced and furious at the barman, which is a little surprising given I am paying for his company. It thrills me though. Although perhaps it is all part of the romantic experience, giving off that super intense male main character alphahole energy – major obsessive stalker about his lady love and all that.

Jai looks stonily at the barman, "Bugger off alright, can't you see this is a date?"

The barman raises an eyebrow, "Wow, okay matey. Now what would ye like to drink?"

We order our pints and sit by the window. Tilting my head I cannot help but ask, "Why did you let off on that barman? We're not on a real date? He might have been the love of my life."

A storm darkens his gaze, and there is a quick hint of a feral expression that sends a hot sensation coursing through me. But then he composes himself and coolly responds while supping his beer, "When we're on Rent-A-Romance time then yeah we are, we're on a date. Do you usually flirt with other people on dates Zasha?"

I look at him sceptically, "I wasn't flirting, and this isn't a real date."

He shrugs, scrutinising me with his cool stare, "Maybe you can't see it but you have this effect on people. Listen, even if there was a boring party, you're the sort of person that just by being there things light up."

I tilt my head and scrunch my lips like don't believe what he's saying, because I don't. My high crime in all of this is to walk into this pub. Now he's talking about me as if I'm some sort of grenade-lobbing femme fatale.

He sees this, takes a sip of his beer and utters hurriedly, "I'm telling you this because you're my client, it's just my professional observation. Take it or leave it."

Narrowing my eyes at him I wonder if he's for real. He's looking away very intently. I let sleeping sea dogs lie and quietly sip on my beer. Mm. It's a good beer, nice smooth flavour on the hops. Looking down into the aromatic, boozy goodness I get the uncanny scorching sensation that I am being stared at. Flicking my chin up, I catch Jai gazing at me with that unfathomable expression again. An expression that has me aching between the thighs. My heart is racing and I am struggling to calm its pace, not even thinking of dolphins frolicking seems to help.

Gazing upon Jai's handsome visage I note that Jai's makeup and goatee are all over the place, like a Mr Potato Head who has been ransacked by an errant toddler. My fingers are itching to do something about it, maybe just to touch him. So I reach across the table in a fashion my mama would tell me off for and I grab his goatee to rearrange its position.

He stops me in my tracks by seizing my wrist, his thumb stroking the tender pulse point, "Careful. You might not want to get too close."

His gaze is severe, looking down at my lips. My breathing hitches, "What happens if I get close Jai?"

Jai's eyes travel back to meet my own. He slowly turns my hand so that my palm is facing upward, the fingers curled inward as a protective reflex. My heart gallops when he kisses the delicate skin of my wrist, then brushes open my fingers to kiss my palm. My belly flutters and a heat rises from within my core.

This must be part of the Rent-A-Romance rulebook. There is no way someone like Jai would want me. Someone magnetic, with a messy charisma. Someone so uniquely handsome that it is hard not to look at him, from the pools of his eyes down to the tantalising 'V' of his abdomen.

Jai seems to have dropped his accent so I clear my throat and get back into character with a bit of flirty banter, "Keep going like this Captain Pirate and I just might shiver ye timber." I prefer to keep up the act, for the fun, but also so we're delineating what's real and what isn't.

I chuckle at my innuendo. He looks at me and gives a lowly, throaty chuckle that makes me want to melt, "Please do. You're quite at liberty to do whatever you like to my...timber," his words lull me into arousal. Then I catch his stare and I realise there is a fire there, and it scorches me, heightening my arousal. Staring I realise that I am transfixed. But this is unhealthy, and confusing, much more confusing than I expected. I didn't expect to feel so muddled by a Rent-A-Romance experience.

Right, I've had enough, "You're just teasing me, I cannot be dealing with this."

My head is spinning with confusion. I am paying him to get romantic with me, and he *is* getting romantic with me, but he is making it a bit too real. It's a headfuck, I don't appreciate it. Even though I paid for it. It makes me feel like a loser, like the only way I'll ever get romance is by being deluded by beautiful men who know how to play me like English cricket; slow and time consuming.

"Okay let's end this. I'm going home," Arising I am ready to leave. It's weird to get the thing you asked for but then find that because it's a fake of the real deal it just makes you feel even worse.

Unfortunately, as I get up I accidentally stomp on his foot. He goes, "Argh!" and hoists his foot up. He then drops his foot down on my foot by accident and I go "Argh!"

As I lift my foot Jai takes ready advantage of my vulnerable balancing act and pulls me to his lap. I cry "argh" in surprise, as he wraps his arms around my waist and playfully says into my ear, "Pirate wench. You're not leaving these here high seas."

He leans in and whispers, dropping the act, "You're not going anywhere, not after what you've done to me…let's just say you've enflamed more than my foot."

"Oh," I quietly exclaim in response, too horny to be anything but monosyllabic.

A molten fire radiates from inner core, setting all parts of me ablaze, hitching my arousal to dangerous levels, wild fire levels. I have also begun to realise that those are not socks in his trousers. No, Jai is a very aroused, hard man. Wriggle a little in his hard lap, I become progressively wetter at the thought.

Jai groans into my ear, "If you do that enough times, I will bend you over this table, and take you right in front of the barman, the randy bugger would probably love an eyeful."

A little moan escapes my parted lips and I lick them as if I were thirsty.

He gently grasps hold of my bun and uses it to slowly tilt my head back towards him before whispering, "I know it's not very romantic to say this, but I very much want to be buried deep inside you."

The way he says it, well it sounds undeniably authentic and I tremble in his arms as his hand strokes my belly. I am wearing this ridiculous pirate outfit and yet it feels like I am naked against him.

It would be impossible to be more aroused, my sex feels so swollen and honeyed that if he were to stroke me with the lightest touches, would I come? Perhaps it would depend where he stroked me.

"Mm…buried treasure, I certainly wouldn't discourage that," I whisper playfully.

He growls, "Not yet. I want you squirming in your bed for the next week until we meet, thinking about the very bad things I plan to do to you. Can you guess what I have in mind Zasha?"

I exhale as I feel his hand travel down and slip underneath my trousers, grazing my knickers. This is so public, I cannot believe what he is doing. It's exciting, but oh so risqué.

Here we are, in a pub, and as a pirate sitting in the lap of another randy pirate. This is all so obscene, "Mm, let's see. What would a naughty pirate dream of? Polishing that cutlass perhaps?"

His hand presses my belly, drawing me even closer to him, "Listen to you, so dirty. I bet if I plucked those panties of yours aside, I would discover that you are one very wet, very horny girl. Am I wrong?" Jai says silkily in my ear, his breath making me shudder.

His fingers go lower still, slipping underneath my knickers. I gasp – the barman looks across the bar at us, narrowing his eyes in suspicion. Jai sees this but doesn't care, he is such a deviant.

"Jai, this is very public," I say, but not willing to budge from my place on his hard thighs, and hard…other parts.

"And you're enjoying it, bad Zasha," he chuckles lewdly, "So will I see you next Sunday?"

"Yes," I say meekly.

"Good girl," Jai's fingers tease the rise of my mons, while the barman pirate polishes the bar in full view.

The barman pirate looks over at us contemptuously and then throwing his polishing cloth on the bar, he saunters over feistily,

"Hey, take it somewhere else the two of you."

The barman's face contorts in a vexed expression, "You have terrible taste in pirates," he hisses at me.

Jai gets up and squares up to him, "Oi, back off my wench would you?" Not sure if wench in this situation is a term of endearment, or perhaps indicates a somewhat wayward woman? I like to think both.

The barman defeated replies, "Argh!"

Jai responds with equal ferocity, "'Argh' back to you too you fucker!"

Then looking at me he takes hold of my hand, "Come on Zasha, let me take you some place with better pirates."

I look at my watch, "I've got to go meet my girls in an hour – sorry Jai! But…"

Looking him up and down, undressing him with my eyes I drawl, "You can hold that thought…or anything else that you desire, for next week."

Usually, I would not be so bold, but something about Jai makes me feel so ridiculously lusty that I lose my head. It's like being drunk. Anyway, it's all good, by pretending I am alluring, he is just doing his job very well. His erection? Easy, Viagra. The guys just a professional, that's all. Just a professional.

CHAPTER 5

Jai

Okay, so I nearly massively lost control there. I just wanted to pin Zaha down and then kiss her, grind into her. I didn't want that sod of a barman coming anywhere near her. Bloody pub pirates. Anyway, I gave myself a massive pat on the back for taking one for Team Patience and allowing myself to waddle to football with frosty balls. All the while being taunted for looking like a pirate by crazies on the underground tube transit.

To bring my raging erection to heel I keep thinking of the least sexy things, like Valley Green Football Club's surprise loss to the Lands Bottom Rovers owing to an own goal. That was shit. I keep that thought on a loop until I am very much tamed down under.

Later that evening I go and play casual football with the lads. It's a weekly ritual and gets us together. The best of them are Deano, Matt, Ademola and my best mate Hunter. There are other guys in our team, but they're cocks; I can take or leave them.

After the footie, the whole team relaxes by visiting a friendly massage parlour. Sounds civilised, don't it? Well just to give you a hint of the nature of the parlour it is called Tantric Touch Adult Massage. Some of the lads like to go all out with the 'full body' massages. Me and my good chaps keep away from the dirty stuff, but still, we pop along for a sports massage; their clean offerings are dirt cheap.

Deano, Matt, Ademola, Hunter and I always go into the same

room so we can have a lark.

But today, it's not the same. It feels depressing in all honesty to have uninterested scantily-clad women oiling us up. Not when I've met sexy Zasha. Now if she was doing this massage…

It also doesn't help that Deano, Matt and Ademola are squabbling about a girl they all like, they always end up going for the same woman. It's quite sad really, but entertaining to listen to. Face down on massage tables, being attended to by nearly-naked masseuses they go at each other.

"I knew her first Ade, you only asked her out on a date because you knew her through me," Deano complains.

"Nah mate. I liked her before you did. You weren't even interested in her like that until I told you I was," rebuts Ademola.

Matt settles the matter "What you two wastemen talking about? She didn't even say yes to either of you. Went with me instead innit?"

And they keep going like that. Hunter and I say nothing.

We hear the door crack open and everyone tenses, even the masseuses. The familiar sharp clitter clatter of stilettos and harsh attitude looms. Miss Harbotham comes sauntering in, dressed accidentally on purpose like a sexy correctional officer. She doesn't so much own the massage parlour as she does rule it. She has a red bob, lipstick and glasses. Gazing daggers at us she pouts in contempt.

"Ah look my cheapest customers, how wonderful to see you. Who doesn't love a virgin? Ah, that's right – me," she says derisively.

Miss Harbotham is always trying to bully us into purchasing one of the pricier services that involves a 'happy ending.'

"We're not virgins," Ademola smugly corrects her.

Miss Harbotham slow claps mockingly and then leans over in front of him. Her large breasts dangles right in front of

Ademola's eyes. He looks hypnotised as they gently sway, "Clever boys. Some poor girls have taken pity on you out there and you didn't even have to pay? Well done…but I meant your Tantric Touch virginity. You are like soft, squishy, white bread virgins to us…you fill the place but you're not very healthy for our growth. Not like your other little footballer friends, now those men, they like a *proper* massage."

Hunter says in earnest, "If you don't like it, then put up your prices for your legit fare."

"Oh I might one of these days, I just might," Miss Harbotham threatens.

Deano coughs, "You're making us all tense."

Miss Harbotham then whacks her palm down flat next to Deano's head on his massage table. Deano squeaks in surprise, "Your insolence does nothing for you here. Many of our men have a happy ending, but there are a select few who have a sad, sad ending. Do you see?"

Is that a mortal threat? Either way, Deano gulps and nods.

Miss Harbotham then straightens her back and looks at us derisively, "Well good night my little red-cheeked virgins."

"Wonder which cheeks she's talking about," Matt tries to joke. None of us laugh. She's got us all tensed again and in knots.

Not relaxing at all. Next time I'm going to recommend to the lads that we peel off from the rest of the football herd and head to the pub instead of Tantric Touch.

We scarper as soon as we're done. There is silence among us as we walk down the street. We're heading towards my Dad's greasy spoon cafe like we usually do after football. It's our ritual, my Dad always fixes us up with the best Singapore chilli crab. My mam used to make that.

Deano is usually the noise maker but after our disquieting massage he is being ponderous. His head hangs deep in thought as we walk. What a depressing Miss Harbotham-shaped cloud we have hanging over us.

"Lads, you alright? Deano – you alright mate?" I ask.

He looks miserable, "Yeah, I just find Miss Harbotham proper peng is all."

Ademola stares at Deano as if he is mad, "What you talking 'bout? She was right ready to chop your balls off and serve them back to you on sticks."

"Yeah, it's fucking sexy," Deano glumly replies. The mysteries of the heart.

Matt looks at me as our dejected lot continue to amble down the street, "What about you Jai? You've been quiet."

Can't help but tell them, "Met a girl today. She's nice."

I am trying to play it cool but I want to shout like a fucking hooligan, *SHE IS BLOODY FANTASTIC!*

"Yeah?" Matt asks with an inquisitive expression written all over his face.

"Yeah," I say, and leave it at that. The lads look at me curiously but know it is best not to pry. I haven't told them about my Rent-A-Romance side hustle because that would open up a can of worms where I would then have to explain my awkward living situation with Nellie. Then they would ask why I don't stay at my Dad's, and I'd have to tell them about my even more awkward situation with my step-mum. Not even my Dad knows about that.

After going to my Dad's cafe with the lads, I travel back home on the bus. When I return to my house I manage to dodge Nellie and crawl into bed. Fumbling in my desk drawer, I find the paper copy of Zasha's profile from Hamish. Just looking at her grainy profile picture, a heat envelops me at the base of my spine, my cock stirring. God this girl does it for me. Dunno if the customers know that Hamish has these profiles of them, but he gives them to us just so that we are familiar with their basic details. Appraising her gives me immense satisfaction, like someone is feather dusting my chest, belly…and well, the obvious. Her picture seemed cute before, but now it is scorching after our encounter.

Pumping moisturiser from my bedside into my hand a buzz of anticipation swells in my chest. Trying to hold up Zasha's picture with the other hand I start stroking my cock while firmly gripping my engorged shaft. This lo-fi way of beating myself off is a bit desperate but I don't give a fuck.

The Zasha in the picture is smiling in a friendly, unassuming manner. Her doe-eyes are framed by glasses. She isn't even wearing a cleavage top, she's wearing a red turtleneck, but that is more than enough fuel for the fire. She is so unassuming, like a shell waiting to be pried open and gorged upon.

Gripping my cock, I caress the length, trying to imagine what it would feel like to have her move against me. Her breath on my neck, tender kisses on my cheek. Picking up the pace I stare into the photo, my hand quivering. I struggle to hold both the photo and my erection so I put the photo down and close my eyes. I try to really picture her; the smile, her gasp when I kiss her, those delicious curves that captivate my breath like a boa constrictor.

Recalling Zasha on my lap earlier, I stroker harder, faster. Thinking of Zasha pressed against my aching hardness makes my cock swell in my fist, precum oozing, drenching my cock in slippery wetness. As I grip my shaft -stroking it- my cock becomes more sensitised. I try and imagine it's Zasha gripping me; milking me. The pleasure grows; like a lightning bolt wrapped around my cock, getting charged, ready to burst. Soon the dam bursts and my cock contracts from the uncontrollable overflow, spurting hot cum into my hand, coating my palm.

Breathing heavily I smile gratified and look up at the ceiling. Lucidity returns in pulses, and the fog of horniness recedes, for now. For now I am not obsessing over Zasha.

Yeah, lucidity is definitely returning. Great thing I can now think of other things. Not just Zasha.

Yup…definitely still not thinking about her. That would be ludicrous. My horny little pirate wench.

I wonder what Zasha is up to right now, if she's touching herself at the thought of me. At one point today she was quite pissed off by how much I was teasing her. I like to think it turned her on… frustrated her.

God it's going to be a mess under my duvet. Too bad Zasha isn't here for me to cum in her, on her…with her. Yanking a tissue from the old Kleenex box I wipe up the sticky evidence of my nefarious activities and then lazily roll to the other side of the bed.

Even as the fuzz of my lust for her clears as it obviously has - my thoughts become clouded with nagging doubt. What is she doing, who is she with? She better be single. What if she's not?

Fuck, never mind my duvet being a mess, *I'm* a mess. Wanking off has not helped my thoughts at all with Zasha.

Finally, I conk out and make my way to the land of nod.

Zasha

Walking to the pub to meet the girls I am floating on cloud nine, maybe even ten. So much so that I don't care when someone wolf whistles and inspired by my attire, enthuses that they would let me wank their plank. Sigh. I mean, come on, what do they expect me to do? Go, *"Yes please rando on the street shouting disgusting obscenities! Take me now!"*

Anyway, I meet up with the ladies at the pub; Lilly, Soraya, Arti and Nat…AKA the Awkward Squad. We've known each other since secondary school in North London. We were the misfits that used to huddle together in the library, reading romances while doodling our favourite characters. We meet whenever we can to catch up. It's fascinating to reflect on how much our lives have evolved.

Lilly wraps one of her red locks around her finger as she looks at me dreamily, "Ooh, loving the swashbuckling chic darling."

I plant myself in a spare chair, "Cheers ma dears. How are you girls doing? Did I miss much?"

Soraya nods leaning forward, "We're all right. Lilly here was just telling us how she went star gazing to see the Northern lights for one night, but she managed to sleep through it all."

Lilly appears pained, "Don't make fun Soraya darling, I was most excited. So excited I didn't sleep the days before I was due to go, and of course dozed off at sunset and missed the whole riveting experience. But it's quite alright, I went on other adventures. Norway, Denmark…ate my way through Denmark."

Her expression softens, as if the cinnamon rolls of Denmark made missing a once-in-a-lifetime experience utterly tolerable.

Arti looks at me with an intense expression. Arti Patel, rebel lawyer without a clause, "Our Lilly's not the only one who has been galivanting. Hey Zasha, how was, what the fuck is it called? Bent-Back-Romance?"

She's being cheeky on purpose, I correct her, "Rent-A-Romance. You know exactly what it is called you deviant."

Lilly leans in, "Do tell darling, how was your Rent-A-Romance experience? We all want to know."

A memory of Jai's warm, large hand cupping my posterior shudders into view like a mirage. With delicious reveries of Jai groping me, my face instantly reddens.

"Ooh! She is blushing! Tell us girl," cries Nat.

Nat is an ophthalmologist which is appropriate as she is the most eye-catching person you ever could meet. She is wearing a yellow top and blue suit, like a sunny day. Her hair is in twists tied to a bun up her head and pinned in place with a felt rose. You would, well, need an ophthalmologist not to notice her.

"Yeah, it was good. Very good. His name is Jai and he is… incredibly dreamy," that kiss we had earlier, then later, the sensation of his hardness pressed against my back…oh it was a dream alright, an incredibly wet one.

Arti snorts, "Still cannot believe you are wasting all this money on someone to pretend to like you. Doesn't that feel a bit lame?" she kicks back and stares at me defiantly, as if she is trying to burn out my psyche with lasers.

"Yes, I mean no," I say thoughtfully, "It feels so real, kind of confusing. So far it has been a scrappy experience, but worth every penny."

The girls look at me with great interest. I don't tell them about all the groping, because well, I'm not quite sure how to slide that into the conversation.

Soraya raises her glass, "Well you're a great advert. Haven't seen you look this happy about seeing a man, in well, forever. Even if it's all pretend."

That thought does make me feel sad, but maybe using Rent-A-Romance will somehow manifest a proper romance by opening my mind to all the men out there? Who knows. Anything can happen.

CHAPTER 6

Jai

The next day I visited the Rent-A-Romance office in the evening after work.

Hamish has convened the usual Monday night meeting with the different Romancers. This is the first time I've attended.

Rocking up to the office I see ten guys all ridiculously buff, tattooed and tall sitting on the sofa's that flank Hamish's desk. They're a bunch of different ethnicities – but eerily samey-looking. Perhaps Hamish has an evil lab somewhere where he brews up beefcakes. I am the odd one out for looking comparatively human. Maybe one day I'll find myself kidnapped off the streets of London and forcefully transformed into a romancing beefcake of the Hamish-endorsed variety.

Feeling self-conscious I tuck myself into the corner of a squishy sofa, sinking so deep in that I'll need to be excavated out. A Mediterranean-looking guy; tattoos, muscles threatening to split his black clothes, piercing green eyes, tan like Ronseal – decides to perch himself right next to me. His arse muscles must be like a chair attached to his bum because he towers over me…or maybe I'm hunching in embarrassment for not having steroids for breakfast, lunch and dinner.

Fuck knows.

They are chatting to each other, obviously proper mates, they don't even notice me. I sit there friendless like a problem child in the corner.

A guy with blond hair that pales in comparison to his mahogany-rich tan looks at me curiously with his extremely blue eyes. I am transfixed by his beauty and the unlikely depth of his hue. I'm as straight as a ruler, or at least I thought I was.

Like a horny bear he growls at me, "Hey fellas, we have a new guy. Who are *you*?" he says with the derisive tone of a prince at court who has had his space sullied with a grubby peasant.

Squeaking out like a fan girl at a K-pop concert I respond, "Me? Uh, I'm just Jai. Uh. Yeah."

The chap arches a brow, "Just Jai? Where's the rest of your name?" he laughs heartily to himself. The others follow his cue sycophantically and soon the room is filled with booming, mocking laughs.

I ignore being the object of their fun, "Yeah alright, alright. So you all the other Romancers then?" I ask.

"I suppose we are all that there is. I am Magnus by the way," he walks towards me and nearly has his crotch grinding my face. He then presents one of his paws.

I shake it – I am not sure if he is just very strong or a right dickhead but he nearly crushes my hand in his grip, "Magnus… that your real name?"

Magnus just seems like a proper porno name.

He looks taken aback, "What else would my name be?"

Magnus sizes me up, "Hm. We could do a reverse harem together one of these days you and I."

Oh man, that sounds like he wants to get his leg over. My expression must have that written all over.

"*Not like that*. A straight man's reverse harem. Dear Lord man, do you not read romances? You'll need to, to survive in this line of work. The women that come through the doors love a good 'why choose?'"

"What does that mean? 'Why choose' what?" I ask Magnus like a true newbie. I don't get it. Maybe I'll take him up on his suggestion and read those romances to understand what Zasha is looking for.

With great pity Magnus assesses me, like when you see an extra hairy cat stuck in the rain, "Jai, wise up to this business, otherwise the boss will take advantage of you. He is devious, and a genius – like the god Odin himself, watching over us here in Midgard – stoking the hearth of human inspiration, as we lay waste to puny cities."

The guy sitting next to me chuckles and shakes his head, "Magnus, you have been playing at the Viking barbarian for too long."

Magnus stares at him derisively, "So says Roman the Roman. Playing the gladiator for two years straight. This guy once tried to jump into a lion enclosure in a zoo to fight it with his bare hands."

Roman leans over to me, "Being a Romancer stuck in a role can send you doolally."

I smile at this. Then I wonder, how do you know when you're in too deep, do you even know? It would be great to know what these guys have been through.

Then just when I am looking forward to finding out more about the other guys Hamish comes lurching in. He has a cigarette in one hand and an oxygen tank in another – spluttering away.

Pretty sure it's illegal to smoke at work, but that's the least of Hamish's many problems.

"Hello Romancers! Good to see ya, good to see ya. Now tonight I don't have much to say other than we have our Christmas dinner in three weeks, don't forget that. Got us a nice sweet spot in a gentleman's club, 'Lapdance in Lapland' is the name of the menu," I grimace. It sounds gross, and the only guy here who looks desperate to have his Christmas supper at a strip club is Hamish.

Magnus catches my averse expression, "Something to say Jai?"

"Yeah. It's weird to be having pigs in blankets while watching a prancing naked lady. No offence or nothing."

Roman looks at Hamish, "What this Jai is trying to say is that he doesn't want an erection while he is having his work supper."

These guys.

Clearing my throat I elaborate, "Honestly, lap dancing clubs don't do it for me. Can't we go somewhere normal, where we don't have to eat the festive canapes off someone's belly button?"

Hamish scrunches his whole face at me, "Nah, we're going. I have a favourite girl there see, Caramel Love. She's gonna be my next baby mama. You guys are just tagging along for the ride."

Rolling my eyes I shake my head.

Hamish throws me a piercing look, "Anyway other than that, for the most part nearly all of you did swell today. So Magnus, guess what? Got an email from one of your clients who has asked to marry you. I said sure, if she's willing to subscribe to more sessions. I'll even throw in surprise baby quadruplets as a free trope. You're doing well son, proud to be your father," Hamish goes up to Magnus and pats him on his steely shoulder lovingly.

Magnus is Hamish's son, how can this be? The only things that I can envisage lurching out of that man's gene pool are an old boot and a flying octopus.

Magnus nods, "Thanks Dad."

Hamish continues, "Kwame, so Magnus is gonna be taking over your African King gig. For a while you're gonna be a black billionaire toyboy cop. We've got a girl keen on it."

Kwame looks at Hamish like he's crazy, "No girl who calls for an African King expects Magnus, even with his new tan. No offense my friend."

Magnus shrugs, "None taken."

Hamish continues, "It's all in the back story. He was a white baby abandoned in the jungle by his explorer parents who decide that they hate having kids. Raised by a leopard who is tragically killed by an elephant he is then found by tribesmen who raise him as their own. But…he grows up to become an alpha male, takes over their village and proclaims himself their chief. Good story right? Seamless."

Kwame shakes his head, "No, bad story. Senseless. Very insensitive. Hamish. Again."

"Fucking fuck you Kwame! Shut that gaping pie hole, unless you want to go back to selling pet insurance over the telephone," Hamish shakes his oxygen tank at Kwame.

Hamish composes himself and stubs his cigarette out on the arm of his armchair, "Okay we're done here. Just a short update for you fellas."

I turn to leave with the others but then I hear Hamish say, "Ho ho ho! Not so fast for you Jai. We're gonna have a word."

The dread of being alone with Hamish courses through my veins, "Yeah alright."

Hamish perches himself on a sofa, "Sit down there, down there Jai."

He points to the sofa opposite.

Sinking into a pit that was previously made by Magnus's steely bottom, I hunch to try and better look this wily old man in the eye. Let him know he doesn't get to me.

Hamish smirks and then produces a paper. It appears to have lots of ratings on it, like a survey. Oh wait, *it is* a survey. Intrigued, I raise an eyebrow, "What's that?"

Hamish shakes it, "That my friend, is the stench of failure. The putrid feel of a woman's disappointment. The scent that greets me whenever I go to my divorce attorney's office."

"Oh right," I respond warily. Can't be Zasha, not by the way she was grinding herself against my lap, goading me with her body.

Hamish licks his lips like the sly old goat he is, "Take a look, proof is in the pudding."

The first bit heartens me, five stars on looks. Nice. I let out a single chuckle at that.

Everything else – well fuck off – she's one-starred me! I mean, what the fuck? A dark storm descends.

"Turn it over, read the comments at the back," Hamish urges, relishing my irritation.

Choice phrases jump out.

"Ripped my dress open…"

"…Made me look like a pirate"

"Didn't read the whole script…"

"…Floppy parrot."

Fucking bag of dicks that is. How can she say all that? Zasha seemed so kind and sweet. Turns out she's a wily she-devil.

"I ripped her dress open because she was wilting!" I protest. Surely Zasha recognized that? And didn't read the whole script? It's because Hamish didn't give it to me! There were pages missing.

Hamish chuckles, "Yeah, yeah. Buddy, don't be a wise guy."

"So what, she doesn't want to see me anymore?" weirdly my heart pangs at that very thought, all I want to do is see her again.

Hamish shakes his head, "Nah Jai, she wants you, she wants you. But we're at the last chance saloon, okay? Take that pain and channel it into being a sexy beast. Here – "

Hamish hobbles up to the desk and pulls something out of a drawer. It's a clear, stuffed packet that says "Dark Romance" on the front.

"Open it," he hisses – like I'm being asked to undo his zipper. My skin crawls so far back that I threaten to become an anatomy project.

Inside of the packet there is a very dubious costume, a rubber knife, and temporary tattoos with a heart and arrow going through inscribed with something that says "J's Fluffy Stuff."

Scrunch my nose, "What are these, temporary tattoos? Where's the rest of my name?" I question.

"Thought 'J' with just one letter was your name," Hamish smirks.

Wanker.

This man needs a reality check, "Mate, seriously - do you know anyone who has a single letter for a name?"

"Yeah, I do, you. Let her be J's Fluffy Stuff, let her have her moment. She'll love it. Hey, she's the one that requested this," Hamish looks self-satisfied as he leans back in his seat, interweaving his fingers.

"Still don't get it. Why would she want my supposed single-letter name on her?" maybe I just don't get girls.

"Hmm, boyo you are gonna need to read some dark romance books."

I look at Hamish curiously, "What's dark romance? Like horror books with kissing?"

Hamish gazes at me pityingly, "Kinda. Let's cut to the chase, we're talking smut so grimy the cops would call you a sick fuck. But you're feeling so smutty and grimy after reading this type of thing you'd beat yourself off to being called a sick fuck right there in front of the cops while knifing someone in the throat."

That's shocking if what Hamish says is true, "No way, Zasha can't be into that?"

"You read it, see how you feel. It's like Viagra – you'll get hard and nasty," Hamish says merrily.

The thought of Hamish getting a stiffy is enough to make my visual cortex explode.

He continues, "This Zasha chick, she is gonna be getting some real kicks from reading this stuff, believe you me. Especially if you bust out that Eastern European accent, call her sweet nothings, like *babushka*, that kind of thing," Hamish rubs his hands in glee.

I pull out the costume, "No fucking way am I wearing this mate, I mean what the fuck? Nah. I'll find something else to wear."

"No, you won't. This was a real manly look when I was a young buck about town. Got the uptown girls hot in the pantyhose," Hamish says with gusto.

It's more than I want to hear, "Too much information. Hey, what's the point of all of this if she doesn't like me? Maybe she'd prefer another Romancer?" I get a sharp pang in my chest just suggesting that. That's mental, I've only known Zasha all of five minutes.

Hamish eyes me sympathetically, "So yeah, so don't feel too bad Jai. Look, she did say she found you physically attractive right? So what if she rated you one star on everything else? Take that hurt, take all that pent-up vengeance and make the performance of a lifetime out of it. She wants the dark romance? You give her the dark romance."

Hadn't thought about vengeance, but yeah, guess I would like her to know how I feel. Both pumped and dejected I utter, "Yeah, I suppose."

Hamish pats his thighs, "Oh well, I'm going back to *ma casa. Adios hombre*." Hamish then gets up and idles out of the office.

I don't know if he just said all that because he still thinks I'm Mexican.

CHAPTER 7

Zasha

~Dark Romance – The Revenge Story of An Unhappy Chappy~

All week I've been excited to see Jai again; replaying the kissing and the touching, over and over in my head. Gauzy memories of Jai flit into mind; the way he sweeps his long dark fringe away from his intense gaze, that smile that turns my core into molten lava, and will I ever forget that spikey cod piece? It doesn't feel like Jai is acting at all when he is around me. It feels real, perhaps that is a testament to his skills as a professional.

Waiting outside of the studios on a chilly day, I shudder relentlessly in the freezing cold. On the adjacent street, the trees that punctuate the pavements are frosted as if dusted by icing sugar. Perhaps I should be grateful for this as it's the closest we are going to get to a white Christmas.

It could be that my annoyance stems from being so horribly underdressed for this weather and having to wait for the habitually tardy Jai while I freeze my sugar plums off. My afro hair is loose, and I am dressed in fishnets, a black leather skirt with the texture of bin bags and a ridiculously low-cut leopard print top, courtesy of Hamish's sticky reveries. When I was walking to the Rent-A-Romance studios from the tube station my coat blew open and a passing businessman immediately asked about my prices. I whacked him in the kisser with my handbag and then made sure I was properly zipped up.

Jai *finally* arrives wearing a long black coat and a surly face, ten minutes late again. Terrible timekeeping.

Mildly miffed I ask, "Why do you always do that? You're late."

Jai looks me up and down, scorching me with scorn, "What are you going to do? Rate me one star?"

Wow. Attitude….unless, it's part of the dark romance scenario? Now that makes sense. Bad boy, bad mood, sweet loving.

Given I have had a week of pent-up frustration I lick my lips and retort with as much sass as I can muster, "Yeah maybe, you going to punish me for it?"

His eyes, cat-like, bore into my own, "Yeah I am." That sends a chill up my spine.

Well blimey.

Jai seems a bit cross, well this is the one that the Brit School let get away. He's certainly giving the villainy.

He opens the door and with a lecherous one over, his gaze feasts on my body igniting my senses. He snarls, "You have your script? It's going to be a long day, especially with all the add-ons."

A heat pools between my thighs at the thought, "You mean, real sex, not just closed door?"

"Yes, and it won't be gentle," Jai says gruffly.

I nod bashfully, my cheeks blushing.

Shyly I remove my coat, knowing that the flimsy garment is hugging every angle, every curve, even the bits I would rather were squashed into obliteration rather than be placed on display. This doesn't seem to matter to Jai, but then he's paid to be pleased.

Softly I hear him whisper under his breath, "Damn,"

"I mean, it's all a bit flimsy isn't it?" No doubt Jai is enjoying all the goodies wrapped in plastic and on display, but it's still a mildly mortifying number.

"Yeah, it's perfect," Jai then stalks up to me and traces a finger across my jaw, before he cups my chin and forces me to look into his eyes.

He practically snarls his words, "Given I could tear it off with my teeth, I'd rate it ten stars."

His aggressive words tug at my belly, and arouse my core, although I am not sure what his obsession with star ratings is. Maybe this is a horrible new kink.

I whimper at his touch. Then he breaks away, his fingers drifting off with seeming reluctance. Scowling he removes his coat, unveiling his outfit and places on a hat, staring at me.

There he stands, fully revealed.

Suddenly there are peals of laughter that reverberate throughout the room, *my* peals of laughter to be exact.

Jai is dressed head to toe in tight, shiny black leather, with a jacket that reveals nothing underneath but his smooth muscular chest. Diamante studs run along the seams of both the jacket and trousers. Then there is his little leather cap, more studded than the Mr Universe pageant. This is too rich.

Barely composing myself I try to appear as serious as possible, curling the fingers of my left hand while sticking out my thumb and little finger. Pretending my hand is a phone I say in a posh voice, "*Ring ring, ring ring.* Uh-huh, is this YMCA the band? Oh great, do you have your leather guy with you? What, you don't?"

I stick my hand out to Jai as if I am handing him the imaginary telephone, "It's for you Jai, the YMCA want their leather man back and they won't take no for an answer. Trot trot."

Laughing at my joke I double over from mirth.

"Ha ha, hilarious Zasha. But you know what leather represents right?" He stalks ominously towards me, or as ominously as a stud covered in studs can muster.

I try and gather myself, "How we so wrong our bovine friends?"

"No, toughness, strength. Discipline." It is hard to stifle the laughter as he edges closer. Looking around the room I see that it is decorated like a dilapidated alleyway, resplendent with weird scarecrows dressed cheerily as bloodied corpses, trash bags, a street lamp, and a bike stand fixed to the floor. Hamish doesn't spare any expense. This reminds me of my bedroom at university after a house party.

Edging back, Jai closes the gap, his inky eyes fixed on mine. There is an expression of pain etched upon his features. I am certainly curious to see where this game will lead, but before I can break away Jai catches me by the waist, "You my girl need a little discipline and toughness, there is something about the brat in you, so flippant in how you could wrong a man who cares for you *babushka*." He purrs dangerously in an unconvincing Baltic accent. Is that part of his Romancer brief for this session? Probably. Still, I seek out his brown eyes to see if he is serious. He's a terrible actor.

"*Babushka* means 'old woman' Jai," I whisper, feeling his hardness press against me.

He places a finger to my lips to silence me – still speaking in his special accent, "I will never stop chasing you down, obsessing after you, no matter how poorly you rate me. Do you understand sweet Zasha?"

Mesmerised, I nod very slowly.

He then clears his throat, "But I will take your virginity as my revenge. I will be your first."

Whispering I say, "I mean, I'm a virgin if you discount the last ten guys-"

He again places his forefinger on my lips to shush me.

"Did any of those ten guys make you come Zasha, around their fingers, their cock, their tongue? Did they touch you until you were begging for release?"

I shake my head, getting wet with the promise of what is to

come, which with any luck, will be me.

"Then you Zasha are a virgin, of the most ruthless, relentless touch. You're mine…my precious," Jai drawls huskily.

"Okay Gollum, this isn't Lord of the Rings," I quip, trying to lighten the heavy, delicious mood that blankets this room and stifles my breath, making me want to claw my clothes off, his clothes off.

"That is a smart mouth, maybe I need to gag it," He runs his finger around my mouth. Sensitive to his touch I release the tiniest whimper.

Then he leans over and whispers an aside, "'Upvote' is the safe word."

I chuckle, "Of course it is."

With great reluctance I press my hands on his chest to create a distance, "So Jai, this is all sexy, very much so - but can we run through the script first if you don't mind? I want to feel the dark romance."

"Oh alright," He says dolefully. He tries to compose himself by straightening the lapels of his obscene leather jacket.

"Who wrote it?" I ask out of interest.

"Hamish," he says. Oh dear – this will be a corker.

I start reading my script out loud, "I am just a girl, a woman, who has felt the weight of the world within my heaving bosoms ever since I ripened from nymph to unwitting seductress."

Nope.

"Yeah, let's chuck these," I throw my script to one side on the floor, which adds to the authenticity of the dishevelled alley. Jai lets out a single chuckle and tosses his script over his shoulder, before sauntering up to me.

He looms over and wraps his arms around my waist. Then he whispers in my ear, so close that the little soft hairs stand on end, "This *is* a dark romance Zasha, what's going on between you and me, it's a revenge story, a very real one."

I'm confused, but he is staring ravenously like a hungry man, his erection tenting his trousers. I say nothing, just enjoy the performance he is putting on.

"You're a very greedy, bratty girl Zasha, who just can't help but demand more, but what are you willing to give? Perhaps let's start with a kiss," Jai kisses my forehead, then the tip of my nose tenderly before he captures my lips with his own. His kiss is soft and yet urgent. When I moan in response Jai pulls me in even closer, making it hard for me to breathe. His fingers weave into my thick hair, and his tongue presses between my lips, darting in and out like a flickering flame. My breathing rises as I grow both mildly dizzy and ridiculously aroused by just his kiss alone. His scent dances faintly in the still air; leather, cinnamon and tobacco – the latter probably the result of Hamish handling the clothes.

Jai moves his hand from my hair and travelling down my back squeezes my bottom possessively. Whimpering in response, my hand finds the small of his back and pushes him closer. I want more, I want all of Jai.

"Can we take your jacket off?" my voice is hoarse from being lust-drunk. My hands are now trembling at his lapels, ready to peel his clothes off.

"No greedy Zasha, not until I say so," he instructs, his breathing heavy, "I will do things to you that will make you crave me, want me as I do you...that will be my revenge. Do you understand?" His nostrils flare, my temperature rises.

It's hard to give sass to that so I just nod, woozy with anticipation.

"Wait, I've got some stuff, hang on," well, that breaks the spell as he rifles through his pocket. Flinty bits come flying out and then he produces a knife.

"What the hell Jai!" I say terrified. I mean if he's meaning to mug me, I already gave him all of my money the day that I signed up with Hamish.

He brings the knife to my vision, "Ah there's a trick to it. Look – " Jai says with gusto before he runs the knife across his own neck. I scream as blood comes pouring out. Thick, gloopy, and smelling like a delicious breakfast condiment.

He's also very much alive.

"Did you just off yourself…with raspberry jam?" My expression must be one of incredulity because he dazzles me with a rogue's smile.

"Yeah, it is. What? Would you rather I actually pop myself off right in front of you?" he runs the back of his hand down my cheek and with a glint in his eye asks, "Do you hate me that much *babushka*?"

Jai captures my hand and presses the blunt tip into my palm, carving something and making a splodgy mess. He then tosses the 'knife' aside.

I hope this is going somewhere. I mean, I love jam as much as the next girl, but not as a form of body painting.

I bring my hand to my mouth to lick off the jammy goo but Jai captures my palm and brings it to his soft lips. Darting out as sinfully as a serpent, his tongue traces the lines on my palm while sucking off all the jam, the suction of which shoots tendrils straight to my clit, eliciting from my throat a small captured gasp. He looks at me like the devil himself; a light smirk tilting his lips.

Playfully, I grab his hat with my other hand and place it on my head. Ambling backwards slowly while he stalks me, eventually my back hits the studio wall, and soon his hard body is pressing against my own. His hard contours making themselves known to my soft ones.

"Sexy Zasha, I am going to ruin you," Jai's eyes are dancing with mischief.

"I would love to see you try," I wouldn't be so bold like this in real life, but given this is pretty much a role play with an experienced man, I can live all my wildest fantasies with little care of rejection.

Grabbing Jai's lapels I pull him in for a kiss. He moans into me, his body trembling slightly against my own. He then surprises me by seizing my wrists and manoeuvring them above my head, drawing them together before using just one hand to keep them restrained against the wall. Well, well – just as I suspected, Jai has a dominant streak. My heart beating fast and eager to see what he tries next I arch my body against his hardness and he groans; a honeyed sweetness courses to my core at the sound.

With his other hand free he finds my throat, and caresses it with his thumb, "This is what you like isn't it Zasha, to feel possessed? Now are you going to be a good girl and show me what a willing, delicious plaything you are?"

I nod wordlessly.

"Good," Jai gently caresses my throat with his palm as he kisses me and his tongue finds its rhythm against my own. With our kisses our noses rub. Jai raises his knee, edging my legs apart, and then he rubs this hardness between my thighs, the sweet friction catching my swollen nub, stoking my desire for him to be buried deep within me.

I am pinned by him against the wall like a butterfly on display.

Jai's hand leaves my throat and lightly trails down to my cleavage. He finds the swell of my breast and cups it tenderly, his thumb idly thrumming my stiff thick nipple. I moan into the kiss from the promise of what is to come. Jai groans out, "God Zasha, you're undoing me."

His lips then leave my own and nuzzle into my neck, he groans needily, as he grinds his cock -still trapped in his black leather trousers- against my throbbing clit.

At first, the kisses he plants down the length of my neck are tender and sweet, and then with increased ferocity there is a sting to them like delicious burns. He is growing more feral, as if to consume me.

"Oh my god, I want you, want you in me," I manage to gasp out, arching my back into him.

"It's all for you Zasha," Jai groans slowly. Our eyes meet; dilate, open pools. He's not playing, he's not acting – but neither am I. I need him, I want him – and I want stop until he is buried deep inside.

"Now turn around greedy girl," Jai snarls into my ear, the low vibration of his voice resonating through my every aspect. His hands take hold of my shoulders and then gently he turns me round, until I am facing the grubby wall and my cheek is pressed against it.

"Why do you keep calling me that? Greedy?" I mean, it's a little harsh.

"Isn't it obvious, because you're never satisfied, are you Zasha?" Jai purrs. His breath sends shivers coursing down my belly like little electric butterflies.

Well, I have no idea what he is talking about. I am actually quite easily satisfied but I'll play along – this is a dark romance after all, "You can never satisfy me Jai, but I'd love to see you try."

Gazing over my shoulder I catch him smiling rakishly. Jai then produces from his pocket a yellow lolly on a stick, on closer inspection it has craters. Hm, what's all this?

Jai kisses my forehead, "This my dear is a moon on a stick lollypop. Befitting of one who always needs more. Now you are going to be my good little virgin whore-"

I give him side-eye.

"- and suck this lollypop very nicely for me until I tell you to stop. Then you're going to hand it over. Do you understand? Get it nice and wet with that sweet tongue of yours."

Shivering at his words I nod, removing the wrapping before placing the lolly in my mouth and sucking. As sluttishly as I can muster I shoot him smouldering glances as I suck. Jai does a sharp intake of air and gently falls to his knees as if he is about to worship me, his head level with my sex. Our eyes meet.

"God you're beautiful, all of you," he says quietly. My arousal swells as he attempts to peel off my tights before snarling in frustration and then ripping them apart with his hands, my heart races in excitement, and shock. Jai doesn't stop there. He then rips the skirt in two and tosses the flimsy material aside. His features are now animalistic, my heart beats faster from adrenaline as I a gentle unease clutches me in my core at his wild turn.

His fingers part my knickers to one side, and then dancing between my puffy lips he crudely spreads apart the wet folds – unveiling the rigid, sensitive pearl of my clit. Cool air hits between my legs before my hips jerk in surprise when a big warm tongue makes contact with my sensitive nub, prodding at first, then lapping gratuitously.

I nearly buckle, "God Jai."

He isn't gentle. Jai laps away like a mercenary. To steady myself at the onslaught of the dizzying attention I use one hand to weave my fingers through his floppy dark hair, trying to draw him further in as he enthusiastically tastes me. With the other hand, I continue to suck on the lollypop as he instructed but my arm is trembling. Jai lifts my left leg and props it onto his shoulder, before his tongue dives in even deeper, burrowing into my entrance which tightens, as if my core is trying to trap his tongue within its honeyed walls. A cacophony of my moans around the lollypop pursed between my lips fills the room, as pleasure radiates from my nub to my toes with every persistent lap of his tongue.

My right leg unsteadily props me up but I nearly buckle. My

face is burning from the sordid dirtiness of all of this; being in this somewhat grubby room and receiving such attention as I hungrily suck away at the sugary orange-flavoured lollypop.

Releasing the lollypop from my mouth I momentarily gasp, "Dear God Jai that is strong, I'll come soon," his hand snakes up from underneath my left knee -propped up anyway on his shoulder- up to my bottom and clasps my soft curves. This sensation coupled with his lapping, threatens to send me overboard; tipping me into a land of sweet sensation.

As arousal thrums throughout my core, he momentarily pries his mouth away from my sex and groans, "God you taste delicious, I could drink you in all day. Pass me that lolly *babushka*." Jai grins at me, my juices are all over his chin. He knows I despair at his use of *babushka* which is why he is doing it.

Rolling my eyes slightly I pull the lollypop out of my mouth with a 'plop' and hand it over. My chest is heaving as I try and capture my breath after the onslaught of pleasure he has subjected me to.

But Jai has other ideas, and they do not involve letting me have a moment of peace.

Feeling the bulbous head of the lollypop rub slowly against my clit, I cry out when he slowly, teasingly, inserts it within me. Clenching around the head of the lolly, I seek out my satisfaction from the small candy. Jai fucks me with it while his thumb rapidly thrums across my nub.

Feeling the heat build I whimper, "Yes Jai, I'm going to…"

Then he slows down to an excruciatingly slow pace, "No you're not greedy Zasha. Not when you could do with learning how to control your appetites."

At this point I want to lob him with a doughnut.

"Greedy am I? Well you had *better* feed me up, otherwise I will do bad things to you," I mutter darkly.

He then chuckles and then kisses my clit almost tenderly. If ever there was a man relishing being a dick, it is Jai Maddox.

He picks up the pace with the lolly and his thumb, before running his tongue along my upper thigh, is he just gratuitously *licking* me?

Pervert. Sexy, yummy pervert.

That thought of delicious pervy Jai just enjoying the taste of my skin topples me over the edge and I feel myself pulsing eagerly around the lollypop, trying to draw it in as if it were a cock.

Crying out words of encouragement I am at the precipice, ready to leap over the cliff of tasty ecstasy, "Oh my God yes Jai, I am coming! Don't stop! No! Nooo! What are you doing?"

He stops completely just as I am in the throes of pleasure, as I was fluttering around that little lollypop head within me. My swollen core throbs in despair like a butterfly that cannot quite take off for flight as the glowing sensation flowering from my clit is blunted.

Judging from his smile when I stare down at him he has done it on purpose.

I could kill him, if I went to the gym enough I would crush him with my thighs. Instead of turning this fake crime scene into a real one I glower instead.

In a mocking tone, he says quietly, "You're lucky to come at all. I should make you thank me for that one. You know, you come rather easily, or is it just for me? Do I do this to you Zasha, make you so very wet and wild?" My cheeks burn with umbrage. How dare he ruin my orgasm and then make fun of me. One of those things is bad enough. Both of them together should invoke medieval torture.

Before I can give him some swift sass his head dips back and I gasp when his tongue once again seeks out my overly-sensitised clit. Then Jai pulls out the lollypop from within my core and replaces it by working in his squirming tongue deep within my aching walls, as his hands clutch my thighs. I cry out, too sensitive, while contrarily wanting more.

Scrambling away from the delectable and yet overwhelming sensation, I try to push his shoulders back. Jai's tongue withdraws from deep inside me, then he laughs like the devil himself.

"Greedy Zasha, is that too much? I am just getting warmed up." He doesn't look repentant at all, in fact he sticks the lolly - covered in my arousal- in his mouth and sucks. His eyes are burning with an unfathomable expression.

"Tasty, just like the girl," he says approvingly and hands it back to me, "Your turn, I want to see you lick it." I take the lollypop and lick it tauntingly with long slow strokes of my tongue, my eyes on his, his gaze filled with yearning. How dare he leave me in this state, a kernel of desire lodged so deep inside that I feel it will never leave. That just as he so loves to remind me, I will remain greedy Zasha, with an insatiable thirst for everything that he has to offer.

Jai growls, like really growls – and then picking me up -my back to his chest- he hoists me up.

"I think, we both want more of each other, right Zasha? We need to fix that," he carries me across to one of the scarecrows dressed to look like a deceased office worker wearing a suit, tie and little slippers, strewn on the floor in tragic fashion. Jai carefully lies me down across the scarecrow, so that my hips are on top and jutting upwards. Ah, making woopy near the deceased – very dark romance.

"What are you about to do?" I ask a thrum of excitement coursing through me.

Grinning sadistically he says, "This"…as he removes the tie from the scarecrow.

I ponder what is going through his…

Sexy…

Demented...

Confectionary-fuelled...

Mind.

Jai

So, talk about going *off-piste*, or perhaps I should *say off pissed*. There she is, pretending she is golden, like she didn't go and give me a cruddy rating before trotting along over here for a shag. The girl has brass balls, I'll give her that.

My mind is addled with conflicting emotions. On the one hand, I have an itch to scratch; I want to get under Zasha's skin and see the vulnerability, the exposure in her eyes. Understand the woman who would rate me a one-star and yet still come back for more.

But it's not just cold hard revenge I want, I want to turn her into my craven little alley cat. Moaning louder for me than she has ever moaned for anybody in her entire life.

So I have her sprawled on this poor sod of a scarecrow, her cheap skirt from Hamish is now discarded, her tights in useless tatters. That happened when I lost it and tore her clothes off. Her trimmed snatch juts out at me, the hairs glistening from her cum, my saliva – so fucking enticing. She's a one-woman thirst trap.

But if I have it my way, I'll be the one ensnaring her.

"What do you think of restraints Zasha?" I bend down and look at her face, her beautiful visage with her heavy-lidded eyes appears nearly intoxicated.

"Uh, depends. Given your half an orgasm prank, what do you have planned? To tie me to a lamppost, pop a dunce cap on and have a wrathful mob chuck rotten veg at my person?" Some vigour returns to Zasha and her legs start to tense.

It's hard for me to stifle a low chuckle at her cynical reading of my intentions, "No, I haven't quite descended to that kink yet. Nah, instead I'm just going to make you cum so much that you'll be begging me to stop. Can't have those hands getting in the way, can we?"

There is a gleam of dark arousal in her gaze and then she... moans, before clearing her throat, "Yes, I suppose. Upvote is the safe word?" she is rubbish at playing it cool. My hardness strains with what is to come.

"Yeah, 'upvote' is the safe word."

Zasha smiles ruefully, "Okay then, you can tie me up. Have your wicked way with me evil boy."

Judging that her puffy slit is shimmering with wetness it is safe to say this idea more than tantalises her.

I smile and wink at her as her eyes follow what I am doing next.

Gazing down at the scarecrow with its drawn-on eyes and terrified expression I am bemused by its supposedly deathly appearance. It is wearing a neat little shirt and tie and is splattered in smelly tomato ketchup. Ah this fella is going to be my accomplice in crime.

Loosening the tie from the scarecrow I gruffly state, "Lift your wrists Zasha, are you quite alright with me tying you up?"

"Yes, I suppose" she replies quietly, her eyes brimming with need. I wouldn't have thought she'd be my biggest fan after the ruined orgasm, but looks like my girl is chasing the dragon, *my* dragon to be exact.

Tying up her wrists slowly I caress her dark skin as I do. Afterwards I walk round and secure the other end of the scarecrow's tie to the bicycle rack that Hamish has inexplicably fixed to the ground. Zasha is just looking at me with a dangerous aspect of lust crossing her face. She doesn't resist, she just watches and breathes heavily. She is still wearing her top, even as her clothes below her waist lay in tatters. We will have to do something about that, I want to enjoy her in her entirety now that she has surrendered herself to me.

Zasha lies prone at my mercy. But her eyes dance with excitement, her chest rising and falling, her beautiful dark skin shimmering.

Pulling out the fake plastic knife I lick from the knife 'edge' the jam goo. The supposed knife is rubbish, but so are the clothes that Hamish gave to Zasha.

Kneeling astride Zasha, I bask in the view, my cock desperately jutting out, ready for her heat.

"What you doing?" she asks curiously.

"Taking off the rest of your clothes Zasha, it's criminal that you wear them. A pretty girl like you should be naked all the time," I throw her a stern look.

Running the knife along the cheap tat Hamish likes women to wear I find that Zasha's leopard skin top tears apart more easily than butter. Zasha's lacy pink bra is revealed. Hooking my thumbs into the bra cups I nudge them all the way down, unveiling her beautiful breasts. Her dark nipples are such stiff delectable little peaks that I cannot help but run the tip of the plastic knife teasingly around one, and then the other. Zasha moans, wriggling underneath me, the makeshift scarecrow 'pillow' underneath her bottom forcing her hips up. Leaning forward, I prop myself up by my arms so that I don't squash Zasha at this angle. I gently bite one nipple and then the other, letting them escape from my teeth. She gasps, arching her back for more, straining against her ties. Her dark brown tits judder appetisingly as she moves.

My arms still propped forward I crawl towards Zasha's pretty face smouldering with arousal, and kiss her on the lips.

"Why have you put the scarecrow underneath me Jai?" Zasha asks breathlessly.

"You'll see," now I am not exactly Lover of the Year, although never had complaints, but for Zasha, I want to blow her lightbulbs out. In the best possible way. This is where I am hoping that the freaky little scarecrow will be my friend.

I spread her legs and work my way between them. Pulling out a condom from my pocket I rip open the packet before unbuttoning my black leather trousers.

Zasha inhales and murmurs appreciatively, "You are one very hot man Jai Maddox," that she remembers my last name surprises me – and it's weird arousing.

I nudge my boxers down further. My cock springs free, straining towards my belly, a pearl of precum budding on top.

Zasha elicits an appreciative moan. Encouraged I stroke myself, caressing the bulbous head, spreading the cum up and down the shaft. The sight of Zasha restrained, splayed, willing, and wet in front of me turns me on so much that it is almost painful. Our eyes meet and I watch her as I roll the condom on, sheathing myself.

Inspiration strikes.

"Do you like pain with your pleasure greedy girl?" I just about manage to rasp out.

Zasha drawls, "I can handle it," she then smiles in a delightfully slutty way that seizes my heart and cock and gently squeezes.

Chuckling I find the black slipper on the scarecrow and tug it off. She tilts her head with interest. Gently I tap the sole of the slipper against her inner thigh. She moans and bites her lip. So I give her more, increasing the speed and soon she is yelping and wriggling, but she doesn't resist, she doesn't give me the safe word, or tell me to stop. Instead, she seems to spread her legs further apart with a moan, her eyes dark pools as her arms strain against the tie. Sadistically I admire the pink marks of the slipper against her dark skin, "Just a little light punishment for you Greedy Zasha...a little hurt for a little hurt." Every once a while I forget about the survey, but Zasha needs to know that *I know*, and I am hurting, more than her rouged thighs.

She looks confused. She is good at playing naïve, I'll give her that.

Holding the weight of my cock in a gentle fist, I run it up and down her wet slit, enjoying how slippery she feels. Zasha looks at me incredulously, her breathing causing her tits to rise and fall. With much anticipation, I push into her and Zasha arches her back as I work the tip into her wet core, feeling her tightness flutter around me, probably still sensitive from her thwarted orgasm earlier.

"God yes Jai, that's incredible," she pants as she tries to buck against me, her arms tugging at the restraints. Using all of my self-control I restrain her with my hands on her thighs.

I plant myself firmly within her to the hilt, my cock stretching her out, forcing her to accommodate me. God, she is tight, and it feels like she is squeezing around me as if she doesn't want to let me go. I hold that thought and bending down I kiss her, slipping my tongue between her plump lips, deeper, rubbing against her tongue. Fucking her mouth with my mouth.

Then I move within her, pistoning up and down as our hips slap together. It's hard to slow down because I want her so very badly.

"Oh god yes Jai, more of you please," she gasps.

I want to say something but I just descend into Neanderthal-like grunts when I try.

"Strangest…threesome…ever," Zasha breathes out with each thrust from my hips. She means Mr Scarecrow squashed underneath her.

I am so close, but I don't want to cum before she does, so I slow down and leaning backwards go into a kneeling position. Then I take her clit and squeeze it slowly, slowly rubbing the pearly pink nub between thumb and forefinger.

"Oh my god you delicious bastard," she cries out.

"Mm, I don't know Zasha, you're the one overflowing with

nectar, so hungry for my cock. Look at how your body prepares itself for me," teasingly I rub her sensitive nub between my thumb and forefinger, admiring her uncontrollable volley of moans as I then do short, hard thrusts into her, one hand supporting myself by gripping her thigh. She is on the edge, I can tell.

Changing the angle of my cock I run it against that sensitive spot deep within her dripping, silky cunt as I caress her clit with little squeezes, rubs…tormenting that stiff pink nub.

There is cum dripping underneath us, and given that I'm wearing a condom, it's safe to say it's all Zasha's. Wet sweet Zasha, her sex begging for me.

This thought pushes me over the edge. I feel my balls contracting, heavy and hot, ready to cum. But I want to feel her spasm around me.

I lean forward and whisper, "Greedy Zasha, I am going to cum soon. Would you like that? Is that what you have been waiting for, to have your delicious pussy swallow me to oblivion? Would that satisfy a girl like you?" My dirty talk seems to do the trick because soon Zasha is moaning, clamping down all around me, and squeezing like a vice, she milks my rigid shaft. The heat squeezes my balls. I am perilously close to cumming.

Zasha is riding out her orgasm as I grind into her hard, my pleasure building into an impending rapture. Soon the electric communion between us overwhelms me until I spill my seed with hot spurts, stars pulsating into my vision.

Soon we are both spent, although honestly, I can keep going this way with Zasha. I don't want to stop touching her, to be inside her.

We kiss, her arms still strained above her head. She is panting away, struggling for breath, her arms deliciously restrained after she allowed herself to become my wanton little plaything. Getting up, I go to the bike rack and untie her, loosening her arms.

Zasha sits up in a merry daze and shakes her head. She then inhales deeply and gets up with her clothes in sexy tatters saunters up to me, her hips swaying, her cum running down her thighs.

Zasha wraps her arms around my neck and pulling me in she laughs, "Oh my gosh, I swear, that was my first orgasm during sex that I didn't end up giving myself, or faking, you know? That was so…so intense. Mm," She looks at me, her visage hard to read. She looks at me thoughtfully, like she's studying me.

"Yeah well Zasha, you needed it," I say roughly, with as much restraint as I can muster. I can tell I am going to be hard again soon.

"Yeah, I did, and that…that hit the spot, in every sense. Thank you," she says quietly, her eyes sparkling as she catches her breath.

Fuck. Even her thank you is a turn on.

I swallow as I behold her voluptuous beauty. I want to wrap my arms around her and kiss her all over.

With this thought I can feel myself hardening. Dear all that is holy I could go again. But I decide to show restraint, even as my cock rouses back to life.

"So uh, we could do some more dark romance roleplay if that is what you want. Or I can take you out to a blues bar not too far from here, blues seems dark romance enough don't you reckon?" Maybe I can then drill her about why she found me so dissatisfying the last time we met.

She wraps her arms around her breasts; her inner thighs are still rouged from being spanked by me with the scarecrow slippers. Hickeys adorn her neck. A little monster in me enjoys seeing my handiwork. Ooh, Damn, nearly forgot -

"Oh uh, and now I am to mark you," muttering unconvincingly

I rifle within my deep leather pockets and find the temporary tattoos Hamish gave me.

"What's this?" Zasha asks, peering at the temporary tattoos that say "J's Fluffy Stuff."

She looks at me most unimpressed, "Nope. Not having some glaring mark to take to work for everyone to gossip over thank you very much."

Sheepishly I smile. God I really can be a bastard, "Well uh, too late. Your neck," I point to her hickeys, and try to imagine how she would explain that away.

Curious, she walks over to her bag and fishes out a mirror, staring agog at her neck she gasps, "Jai! Why did you do this to me?!"

"Because you're a sexy lady and I really wasn't thinking," I say truthfully, brushing my fringe out of my eyes. Never even gave someone hickeys when I was sixteen. Didn't count on starting now.

"This is going to take ages to go," she complains, running her finger across the trail of marks; evidence of how much control I lost in my frenzy.

I've never really lost it like that before. Honestly, something about Zasha just makes me shed my inhibitions.

"Yeah, I didn't mean to…I was carried away," but the thing is, I would do it again, this time somewhere more discreet. So regrets? The jury's out.

Well if she gave me one-star last time, then for the hickeys alone she is giving me the minus marks.

Ah well, I enjoyed my time with Zasha, even if the feeling wasn't mutual.

Zasha is looking at me expectantly, "Jai…are you going to get me some clothes?"

I smile sadistically, circling her, "Nah, I have a better idea," I crouch down to her eye level and taking her delicate hands gently pry apart her arms, letting her tits spill out, her nipples hard, from the cool air, feeling aroused.

Her breathing hitches.

"Maybe I can keep you here naked, aroused, ready for me. What do you think?" I cup her chin with my hands as her lips part from my words and I kiss her once more.

She looks at me squirming from my words, molten need in her beautiful, large brown eyes, "I mean, you could…"

I laugh at my horny girl, enjoying teasing her, "Or I could take you out for supper and some good blues. Can't keep greedy Zasha starving."

Her eyes widen and she slaps me across the arm, really meaning it.

I want her again.

But does she want me? Not apparently if I have a floppy parrot.

CHAPTER 8

Zasha

Why is he doing this to me? He's blowing cold, then scorching hot. At this point I feel like a crème brûlée. On the one hand, he seems pissed with me about something, but on the other, he kisses and touches me at every opportunity that he gets.

And oh my, the sex…I have never come so hard in all my days. I know he is paid to give this level of pleasure but, it felt amazing. Far more intimate than I would expect from a sex worker, I keep forgetting that's all this is. I need to remember that, that is all this is. Transactional service sex; designed to hook me into paying a very pricey subscription.

Jai got me another remarkable costume; this one is a red and black Spanish Flamenco dancer outfit. He looks pretty pleased with himself when I put it on. I see why, my jugs are threatening to overflow like a shook can of Coke. Considering I am the only one paying for the Rent-A-Romance experience, I feel like he's getting his jollies out of all of this just as much as I am, maybe more so. Not that I'd change that.

He still has that look on his face – ravenous. Every time he looks at me with that hungry expression - like a wolf who sees supper - it sends arousal coursing through me like rivulets of honey gathering between my thighs, pooling to be feasted on.

The new flamenco dress pushes my bosoms nearly up to my chin, it's ridiculous, but Jai seems happy. His arm is wrapped around my waist.

He doesn't say anything though.

It's a dark winter's evening, crisp and edged with frost. Looking up at the impending night sky, navy black like blotted ink against velvet, I spot beautiful Venus, minuscule shards of the glorious star's light catching the eye.

"If there was only one star that I had to have in the sky, it would be Venus," I declare in quiet reverence; reflecting on the universe and how small we are compared to the vastness of space.

A silence befalls, as we surely both contemplate the mysteries of the cosmos.

Suddenly…"What is it about you and your one stars?! You're obsessed woman," Jai growls, his arm tightening around my waist.

Right, gloves off, "Hey weirdo! Me and one stars? It's all you've been talking about since you started this morning. Care to tell me what is going on?"

A sullen expression etches itself on Jai's visage, his long fringe flops in front of his face.

"No…can't," he mumbles.

"Just out with it, okay Jai? It was kind of cute when I thought it was some quirky character acting, but now it's just gone on a bit too long," I huff.

We pass one of London's many alleys. Suddenly Jai drags me into one by my waist and presses me against a brick wall. He's got a hard-on. Again. I don't know how he continuously wields that thing.

It's all rather thrilling.

"You've got some nerve Zasha. Do you get a kick out of this? You know exactly what you did," his finger is stroking the side of my face; clouds of his breath starkly paint the night. Perplexingly he is both annoyed and also sporting serious trouser wood.

"No. I don't, I really don't know what I did," I say simply, my heart is thumping hard against my chest...and yet I only grow more aroused for this surly man. I want to drag him home and keep him in my bedroom until someone gets suspicious of his absence and alerts the authorities. Okay, dark tunnel of thought there.

"Yeah Zasha, 'floppy parrot'...ring a bell?" he asks aggressively. He lets me go and backs off, continuing to walk down the street, I chase up to him.

"No. A euphemism?" Jai would make a great pub quiz master.

Turning around and facing me, he enigmatically leans in and growls into my ear, "Or here's another... 'made me look like a pirate'."

"Can you give me some context Jai?"

"They're your survey comments Zasha! Your survey. Hamish shared them. One star you gave me for nearly everything other than looks. Don't pretend," pained – he confronts me with this, his features etched in distress.

This is so puzzling, "But I never received a survey, Jai. What on earth are you talking about?"

Jai looks taken aback, "Yeah you did, Hamish showed me what you wrote."

"Hmm...oh right. 'Floppy parrot', well who gave you a floppy parrot to wear?" Doing what I can to help Jai see the light I touch his elbow. His demeanour relaxes.

"That's not the point, what about your torn dress? Only you and I knew about that," Jai persists.

"Are you sure, did you share that detail with anyone else, in any way?"

Jai's brows scrunch together, "Other than writing it in the inventory log when I picked up the pirate outfit for you..."

A moment of realisation crosses Jai's face, "Hamish wrote the survey! Fucking dick."

I shrug, "There you go, but even if I had rated you one star Jai, come on, is this how to handle it?"

Jai looks at me in despair, "For a lot of people I would handle it better, but, well, I had fun with you that day…and I like you."

I say nothing. Jai is going deep method with his Rent-A-Romance brief. It's affecting me though, strangely I don't like having my feelings toyed with. I am beginning to suspect this is another way to get me to renew my subscription once my sessions are up.

"Look Jai, I know it's your job to keep me hooked, but if it's okay, can you ease off on acting like you fancy me when we're not doing a scenario, you know? I'm a big girl, I can handle something just being a bit of slap and tickle."

"No." He says, gazing at me for a long time, with a very severe expression. His hands stuffed into his pockets.

"Because I do fancy you. You're incredibly cute, and *so* sexy," he says quite simply, making my heart skip a beat.

He's good, I'll give Jai that. Hamish *has* unleashed a dang pro on me.

I breathe in but don't say a word, we don't speak. Instead, I carry on walking, feeling his stare caress my features under the light of the street lamps.

We get to the blues bar, an intimate place with an old country blues band playing in one corner and people chatting and enjoying their beverages in the surrounding seats. Guitars are dotted about the wall and a blue sheen basks the room in its soothing light. I keep my coat on, feeling foolish for my flamboyant outfit. We find a spare table to sit at in this busy establishment. Jai sits opposite me, his leg twitching nervously. He looks over at another table, some bulky guys are sitting there beckoning him. One guy with blond hair and a tan that goes deeper than the Earth's molten core waves us over patting two vacant chairs at his table.

Jai rolls his eyes and grabbing me gently by the hand leads me over, "They're a few of the other Romancers. Sorry Zasha, I wouldn't have come if I had known they would be here too. Don't worry about meeting them, they're alright."

The blond guy looks pretty pleased with himself. "Sit, you girl can sit next to me. Hmm, I see Jai has you in a dress. You're beginning to make a habit are you not Jai of robbing this poor girl of her clothes?" I reluctantly sit next to the guy, he is sporting a very smug smirk.

"How do you know about that?" Jai asks him defensively.

"The inventory log, it can be very…interesting, to say the least. Don't forget Jai, the rules are there for a reason," the blond guy sermonises.

Jai looks like he is about to say some choice words but has changed his mind, "Cheers Sensei Magnus, what would we do without you?"

"Oh I think we know…now on that topic, Jai, will you introduce us to this enchanting creature?"

Creature? Being called that makes me feel like a beloved pet budgie.

"I'm Zasha," I say and politely hold my hand out to shake his.

"I tell you what you are Zasha, you're exquisite," Magnus smoothly charms. He takes my hand and cups it into his own. Taken aback by the freshness of his moves, my eyebrows jerk backwards.

Jai looks at Magnus as if he wants to set his hair on fire, "Fuck off Magnus, alright?"

"Wow, territorial, have you read the rules Jai? Rule number three, if someone is not your direct client you may date them, and rule number seven, outside of the official Rent-A-Romance locations, the role-playing stops. So you may want to lay off huh buddy?"

Jai's jaw is ticking as if he is trying hard to hold back. Interesting.

I clear my throat and announce, "Okay, I am going to get some drinks, anyone want anything?"

Magnus stands up, towering over me so much I just about reach his belly button, "I'll come and help you." *Um, awkward.* At this point, I wonder if he's just trying to piss off Jai.

Jai gets up and faces up to Magnus, "Sit back down with you alright Magnus? I'll help Zasha."

Hm, there is some friction going on between these two. The intensity could set the fire alarms off.

Jai leads me to the bar where there are a few people in front of us.

"Jai, this is so confusing. You're acting like you're not acting...but we both know you're paid for all of this right? Right? So what is it that you actually want?"

Jai leans over and whispers in my ear, "You. I want you," His gaze is so fierce it is hard to look at him. My heart flutters, I really do want to believe him.

"You don't even know me that well," I say to him.

"Yeah, well I'll get to know you."

Then he asks, "How come you're doing this Zasha? You're so amazing, why would you pay for someone to pretend to want you?"

"Way to make me feel like a loser," I mutter. A loser who is five thousand pounds out of pocket. The crowd thins at the front of the bar as people collect their drinks. We push forward, now pressed against the bar.

"Not trying to make you feel like a loser, but you know, I am the one who should be paying to spend time with you, is all. In all my days, you're the most amazing girl," he earnestly tells me.

Is he suggesting that he would pay *me* for intimacy and sexual favours? Well isn't that just the sweetest thing…I just have to plant one on him. I stand on my tippy toes to reach Jai, tilting my chin and puckering up, and as I do he instinctively cranes his head to meet my shy, tender kiss. His hands cup the back of my head and brush against the tendrils of my hair.

Breaking the kiss I tiptoe as high as I can, my mouth close to his ear, "That's for being sweet, in your own way. Although giving me the orgasm earlier was pretty welcome too," I loudly jest. He smiles a disarmingly sincere smile. A chap standing next to me clearly hears what I just said and turns around giving me a cheesy grin. I shade the guy with one withering glance and clear my throat, my attention turned back to Jai.

Jai brings his mouth to my ear, "It won't be the last Zasha, honest. I would happily make you orgasm all day long, all night long," his voice is so low and controlled it almost sounds like a threat; a most delicious one. The thought of Jai dedicated to the cause of making me climax hardly makes me unhappy.

Finally, the barman takes our orders. Jai orders fish and chips with beers for the two of us. We take the beers back and await our food being brought to the table, although I'd rather not sit next to the other Romancers. It's quite tense and Magnus is a bit too extra for my liking.

We go back to the table all the same. Magnus is leaning back in his chair, looking at us as if he is stewing, "Jai, Jai, Jai – haven't you been a naughty boy? Tut, tut, tut! That did not look like a Rent-A-Romance-sanctioned kiss. My father would certainly have something to say to that."

Father? At first I am confused, but then I twig that Magnus is Hamish's son. This opens up so many questions. What sane woman not on hallucinogenics would get with Hamish and produce offspring? Oh what a caper of a story this must be.

Jai retorts back to Magnus, "Fuck off Magnus, just because I'm doing a better job of being a Romancer than you."

Well, that douses everything with a cold splash of reality. Jai doesn't like me at all, I am just another client to him, and everything he does and says is just part and parcel of ratcheting up scores for his work. For all I know Hamish probably has a gift hamper and a glass of prosecco at the ready for any Romancer who lures the most gullible fool to repeat their subscription. I put down my beers and mutter, "Excuse me."

My heart thumping I leave and walk out of the bar, aiming to put enough distance between Jai and I as possible. I get quite far until I am halfway down the road and can hear Jai shout, "Zasha! Come back!"

Turning around I see that he is running like a loony tune towards me. I pick up the pace.

Jai catches up and tries to capture my waist with his hand, I pry it off, "Get off me Jai! You really don't mind playing with my feelings, do you?" I hiss, hastening my steps.

Jai has no problem keeping up with his long strides, which is irritating. One of his footsteps equals ten of mine.

"Zasha, wait up, our fish and chips are ready!"

"That's quick. Must not make them fresh," I grumble darkly, scurrying as fast as my legs will take me.

"Zasha, what's wrong?" Jai asks in despair.

"Go back to the bar Jai, I'm going home. Alright?" Thar doesn't deter him, he keeps following me.

"I'm coming with you," he sounds resolutely. Well too bad for him.

"What, so you can get another shag out of it? You can mess with my head some more?"

Jai takes hold of my shoulders, "Look, I cannot tell the other Romancers about us. We're not supposed to be improper with our clients."

This baffles me, all we have been is improper, "I don't

understand, but I thought it was okay for you to sleep with clients?"

Jai is quiet for a while, like he is crunching something in his head, "Well yeah, uh, but you know, we're meant to be discreet about it."

I narrow my eyes at Jai, why do I get the distinct feeling he is being shady? I don't like it.

"Good night Jai!" I turn on my heels and abruptly head towards the nearest underground tube station.

"Will I see you next week?" he cries out to me hopefully.

"Who knows? I am sure you'll get your pay day though," I say contemptuously.

There is something off about Jai Maddox, and I'm too damned tired to dwell on what that thing is. He's making my heart hurt.

CHAPTER 9

Jai

Sometimes a chap needs to recognise when a girl isn't having it, and Zasha? She was done. Like done.

But I'm not. She's the hottest girl I've ever met in my whole life.

After all that, I went back home, dwelling on how I could fix the situation. Then I had an idea. Not a wholesome one, but I reckon it will cap off the whole dark romance experience. I am going to engage in some breaking and entering.

The next evening after work, I haul myself to the weekly Rent-A-Romance meeting.

I'm late. All the guys are there, chatting in animated banter. When I come in they go silent, like they've been talking about me. Great to see that brotherhood ain't dead.

With Zasha ignoring me and the distinct feeling that these guys don't like me, I do what I have always done my whole life. I go on the defensive. Fuck them.

"Yeah, that's right, keep talking about me fuckers. I'll just be sitting right here," now because they're all sitting on the sofas I have nowhere to plant myself. So like a kid in school assembly I sit on the floor, folding my legs. Next, I'll be singing All Creatures Great and Small.

Magnus the shit is the first to stick it in, "Nice to see you Jai, but I think you're in the wrong place. This is Rent-A-Romance, Rent-

Boy-Romance is next door."

"Ha bloody ha. You're fucking fun," I lay my head against the wall and close my eyes. It's not great that Magnus has twigged what Zasha and I have been up to. It's only a matter of time before he blabs to Hamish.

"That Zasha is pretty, I like her. It's so sad that Hamish scraped you out of the bottom of the bargain bin for her," Magnus needles. I flip him the bird.

He's obviously jealous that Zasha and I have a spark. But what an aggressive dickhead he is being about it all.

Roman sighs, "Settle brethren. We must save our fight for the world outside the Colosseum."

Poor guy. Too deep for too long.

Thankfully Hamish ambles on, "Hey, hey boys. Good to see ya, good to see ya. How you all doing?"

There is silence as Magnus and I duel with stern eyes.

Hamish doesn't seem to notice, "So let's start with you Kwame. So this week you were a toyboy billionaire cop. How did it go with your girl?"

"If by 'girl' you mean a ninety-five-year-old lady. She kept asking me if I could spare some of my billions to help pay for her retirement home arrears," Kwame says aggrieved.

"Okay, uh. What did you say?"

"I said to her, sure, have some of my billions. Hey, while I am at it, would you like a new stair lift?" Kwame says sarcastically.

Hamish nods approvingly, "Good, good. As long as you didn't kill the illusion, you know."

Kwame rolls his eyes and leans back.

"Hey so Magnus, son – how's the African King scenario going?"

"My date ran away from me when I turned up in the kente cloth robes," Magnus bemoans.

"Oh okay, cool. Sounds like a refund, maybe she'll like herself a billionaire ebony stud toyboy instead," Hamas licks his lips and appraises Kwame.

Kwame shakes his head, "Please no Hamish. Don't call me an ebony stud ever again. Okay?"

Hamish shrugs, "It was a compliment. Geez. Can't even give out those these days. Listen, I call Magnus here a vanilla stud all the time. Okay?"

"That's not okay, he's your son," Kwame interjects.

Hamish ignores Kwame, "Okay. Let's do a round-robin on the rest of your weekly reports."

We each go round and give a report.

When it comes to me... "Yeah, the dark romance scenario was good. Went well. Standard stuff."

Magnus snorts, "If by 'standard stuff' you mean tongue down the throat and getting gropey with her in the blues bar."

"I did not grope her," I protest.

"Yeah, but you wanted to."

What is it with this devil-child? "Fuck off Magnus, just because your date ran away from you; smart girl."

Hamish asks curiously, "Is this true Jai? You getting fresh with a date?"

"She didn't love the script you wrote, so she wanted to try something else," well, I am not lying.

Hamish strokes his chin and narrows his eyes, "Hmmm."

Hamish then waves his hand, "Okay you're all dismissed, except for you Jai."

"It's like detention," I protest.

The others leave. Hamish just looks back and smirks, like the sod that he is.

Hamish spreads his legs.

I clear my throat. There is a certain deception that I need to address, "So Hamish, the survey? It's not real, is it?"

Hamish chuckles; the low sinister cackle reverberates around the room "Oops! Caught. Yeah, you're right. It's just a great way to rile up new Romancers for the dark romance situation. Get you real mad, make the girls think you're really into it, *capiche*? Hey, I'm doing you a favour!"

I scowl at Hamish, "You made me look like a right wanker in front of Zasha."

"Nah, you would have done that all by yourself," He says with his usual gusto.

He leans in, "So what she say when you gave her the rose with the bloody thorns? Girls love that stuff."

"Erm, there was no rose?"

"What!? What the fuck. She has to have the rose. It's the cherry on top of the whole scenario."

Well, that was a stroke of luck, I had been planning to break into Hamish's drawer to get Zasha's address, but this is much easier, "Well, hey I can take it to her, if you give me the address?"

Hamish nods, "Aww, you're a trooper. You go get that girl, and all her money for next month's subscription."

CHAPTER 10

Zasha

It's ridiculous really, because I am still pissed at Jai. Really I am.

But that doesn't stop me from tossing and turning. Spreading my legs and running my fingers up my thighs, recalling those places that he touched. The sensation as he stretched me, filled me to the brim…his arms and body wrapped around me.

My body craves Jai.

My mind thinks he's a dirty dog.

Suddenly I hear a sharp clanging sound directly outside. Then a man cussing. Turning on the bedside lamp I put on my glasses and shuffle to the window.

Blimey, I must be manifesting, for stood there is Jai, bearing a rose?

I mean, why didn't he just use the doorbell? What's he trying to do?

He hasn't seen me yet, so I watch as he saunters to the drainpipe and attempts to climb it, but slips down and falls on his bottom. He gets up, straightens his back and dusts down his green Fred Perry polo shirt like he's trying to style it out. I shake my head and sigh.

I mean seriously, this boy. I don't know if my mother would like him.

I go to the front door to see what he is up to, and low and behold he is standing there. Looming over me with a cheeky smile as he presents me with a black rose that appears to have tomato ketchup smeared on the stem.

"How did you get my address?" I feistily ask, trying to sound tough.

"Hamish, but I would have got it anyway. Can I come in?" He looks around the hall.

"Nah, my boyfriend will have you," I tell him coolly.

Jai appears shocked, like I've struck an arrow through his chest.

One corner of my mouth tugs into a smile, "Come in, it's just me and my housemate Phyllis. She's out at a Jane Austen convention or something."

Phyllis is a historical romance nut. She moved from America to London just so she could go cavorting in the gardens of stately homes at the weekends with other historical romance nuts. She is delightfully ridiculous. Our home is also ridiculous; it has been done up to look like some kind of Victorian brothel. Thankfully the landlord tolerates it, probably because he fancies Phyllis and wouldn't mind if it was a Victorian brothel.

"Wow, the walls are trimmed with tassels. That's brave," Jai is smiling at the décor.

I don't want to take the credit for Phyllis's unique style, "It's all my housemate Phyllis. She's allergic to MDF and modern carpentry techniques."

"And good taste," Jai mutters.

"She has taste," I say in defence, although I didn't necessarily say her taste was good.

Now, with Phyllis asleep, I could take Jai to the living room…or my boudoir.

I open up my bedroom door.

"Come in," I say gruffly. He doesn't need to know how thrilled I am to have him as company.

Jai cocks a lopsided grin, "I've never seen you in glasses. They look good on you. Really good," my cheeks flush as his thumb traces the frame of the glasses. His breath grows weightier and he steps closer towards me.

Trying to regain my composure I break away from his contact. Turning my back to Jai I amble into my room. Big mistake.

His arms wrap around me from behind and he pulls me in, "God you're irresistible."

Jai's nose nuzzles into my neck as the palm of his hand presses my belly, his other hand still precariously gripping the thorny rose. He is dang hard again and pressing himself into the crest of my bottom tantalisingly. Flooded with heat between my thighs I try and keep my head above the water.

"Stop Jai. If you got my address from Hamish, is this another scenario? What's that rose for?" I reluctantly peel off his hands and turn around to stare him in the eye.

"Ah yeah, the rose…Hamish gave it to me to give to you. Dunno, was thinking of leaving it by your bedside after a little breaking and entering, thought that might be romantic," I raise an eyebrow at him. He smiles, his teeth biting his lower lip mischievously. Rent-A-Romance is a bit of a criminal organisation.

"What did you come for Jai? I have work tomorrow," sighing I cross my arms.

"So do I," he looks me up and down with particular intensity.

"This is becoming a head spin. I really don't know what you're looking for. Can you go?" rubbing my forehead with one hand, I use my other to flick my forefinger to the door.

"No," he says.

"No?" I say incredulously. It's my home, he doesn't get to refuse, no matter how sexily he does it.

His eyes bore into mine and he walks towards me, wrapping his arms around my waist.

"No. I like you," he says with conviction.

My breathing increases as his dilated brown eyes drown into my own, before he descends and captures my lips into a kiss, his tongue gently darting in and out; accelerating my heartbeat.

Jai breaks the kiss and says, "I am not going to have sex with you tonight, alright?"

He pulls me in closer and rubs the tip of his nose against mine.

"Cocky that you were assuming I would have let you," I tentatively wrap my arms around his hard, lithe torso. Maybe I'm being gullible, but I just can't help but melt when I'm around him. It's like a warmth in my core that grips me

"Yeah, we're not going to fuck. I am just going to do this instead," he kisses me again, softly. Jai's lips caress mine, like velvet against velvet. His tongue brushes the seam of my lips, before gently prying within and greeting my tongue in laps, tantalisingly, like a slow fuck. My heart rate hitches.

Taking his hands I lead him to the bed. He kicks off his shoes eagerly, and then clumsily removes his clothes, so that he is just in his boxers, his hardness pronounced through the fabric.

I mean, it just seems ridiculous not to use it.

"Are you sure you don't want to, *you know*?" not so much a question but more of a helpful suggestion. I pointedly look at his inviting erection.

"It is all I want to do, but we have time for that Zasha. Tonight I just want to wrap my arms around you, feel you sleep against me," he squeezes my hand in his.

Jai leads me to my bed -a knowing twinkle in his eye- and we clamber on, sliding underneath the duvet. Turning off the light he presses himself to my back as we lie, his body scooping mine, his presence setting me on a pleasant edge. One hand snakes over my waist and a warm glow spreads from where his touch rests. But soon his hand awakens once more, his fingers tracing a path down to my abdomen. Jai's hands slip underneath my pyjama bottoms, beneath my knickers; my breathing hitches in anticipation as the tips of his fingers dance just above my cunt.

"Do you like this Zasha, when I touch you here?" he moans, his fingers dallying just above my clit.

"You know I do, you wily tease," I thrust myself back against him. I rotate my hips in a desperate attempt to meet his fingers.

He draws his fingers slightly away, playing with me, "Greedy, needy girl. No manners at all, you should ask nicely Zasha."

Panting a little, I plead impatiently, "Are you running a fishing school now? Give me what I need Jai, or I swear, I will jump your bones," I slightly move my hips up to his hands suggestively. Jai chuckles and plants a lingering kiss on my neck.

"Don't worry greedy girl, I'll give you what you need," Jai's words drip with longing.

His forefinger dips further down and rubs my nub, setting me alight, little sparks course in zig zags from my very core. His lips then find my earlobe and tug, I moan loudly. He groans at the sound of my pleasure.

"God Jai, I thought you said we weren't going to have sex," I moan, my words blending as I lose touch with the world of lucid realities and harsh things, and slip into the realm of the sensual and wispy.

"This isn't sex Zasha, this is me enjoying every inch of your glorious body. Allow me this," his voice is thick with arousal. Jai rubs my clit roughly, his breathing ragged in my ear. He then dips into my drenched core, to lubricate my swollen, stiff nub with my wetness and spreads it. A warm aura of pleasure besets me and a low, needy moan escapes my throat.

"What else do you like Zasha from your pervy dark romance

books? Hand to the throat, or over the mouth as you cry out? Making you cum as you go to sleep? What does it for you Zasha, my sweet sexy freak?" he says. I mean, all of what he says should be deeply offensive, but instead, his taunting makes me wet.

"All of the above," I say meekly.

He chuckles, "Sweet sexy freaky greedy Zasha."

"That's a long, long thing to call me. Just call me Zasha."

"Zasha…Zasha," Jai strums my clit like he is playing a song between my thighs as he casually plants kisses along my neck and presses me against his thick hardness. This could drive me crazy, he could drive me crazy. He places his hand gently at my throat and strokes it's length with his calloused thumb.

The sensation builds, and as it does, so do my moans getting louder and louder. This time he isn't cruel as he was during the dark romance scenario. He doesn't stop the crash of pleasure as it overwhelms me, as I cry out, squeezing his hand between my thighs. He dips his lips to my neck and kisses tenderly as he rubs his cock against my lower back.

Jai bites my earlobe, and a good hurt radiates through my body like a shock of warmth, eliciting a throb, prolonging the cascading orgasm that crashes, and crashes and burns, searing ecstasy from my clit, fanning throughout my core. I cry out his name again and again, gripping my duvet as if it were an anchor.

"Have you come for me Zasha? You're soaking wet," he whispers in my ear. I can hear the smile in his voice. He knows I have, he is lying next to me, so of course he can feel the aftershocks, the shudder that wracks my body…and yes the come that drools from my cunt. He's taunting me.

"Uh-huh," I yawn, rubbing myself against him like a cat on heat. He's still hard; just the thought tantalises me. But my eyelids… slumber is descending hard and fast.

I am getting sleepier. Jai withdraws his hand and kisses the nape of my neck tenderly.

"Rest up Zasha, how would you feel about me continuing to play with you as you do?" he asks.

"Mm, that's a welcome proposition," just in case he is in any doubt, I press my bottom against his unsatisfied hardness. God that erection.

Throughout the night I feel him rubbing, squeezing, kissing, enveloping me in his bubble of arousal. He doesn't stop touching me, my cunt feels like a swollen fruit. I am so aroused and wet between my thighs that I worry about drenching the bedding.

The next morning I reach out and his side of the bed is hollow and cold. But at least he left a note *"Had to go back home to change for work. Here is my number. Don't lose it!!"* Smiling, I roll out of bed and stretch. I still feel the throb within.

I get ready for work, smiling like a simpleton.

Jai

Returning home the next morning to grab clothes before work I am grinning ear-to-ear like a loon. As soon as I get through the door I am immediately caught by Nellie.

She's wearing red lacy lingerie and sticks her tits out at me. It is nothing but irritating. I ponder when I will have enough cash to quit this pile.

"Hey Jai, what are you up to? Where did you go last night?" Nellie steps towards me, trying to wiggle her hips sexily. I take two steps back.

"Nowhere that you'd care about," dodging her I walk past down the hallway.

In the last couple of weeks since I started at Rent-A-Romance Nellie has been acting differently, attempting to flirt in her own crazy way. The other day she left a condom in the fridge with a post-it note that said "Nellie Hearts Jai". She obviously senses that something is up. Her tops are getting lower and lower, and skirts getting higher and higher. Soon she will be prancing around in nothing more than a belt.

"Well, I could have put the bolt on the door so that you wouldn't have been able to get in. That's the sort of thing that can happen when I don't know where you're going, and then where would you be? Sleeping outside I suppose!" I take that to be the threat that it is.

I don't feed her beast. Shrugging, I wander into the kitchen and grab cornflakes and milk.

Nellie follows me, "I'm serious. I can't have you coming in all hours of the night. For all I know you've become a serial killer."

"Yeah well, I have a nice bowl of cereal I'd like to kill before I go to work," I mumble. I need to be more careful around Nellie. She uses everything against me in the end.

"I'll report you to the police," she threatens, baring her teeth.

"Go ahead, they love having their time wasted," chewing my cereal I try to avoid eye contact by doomscrolling my phone. However with Nellie fussing around me I've lost my taste for the most important meal of the day.

Deciding to get dressed for work I set my bowl of cereal to one side and make my way to my room.

"This isn't over Jai, I'll find out what your sly charva arse is up to! Don't think I won't," she threatens. Her eyes are twitchy and nostrils flared. I shake my head. Man, I need to get out of here.

The thing is, I also want to give Zasha her money back.

It's wrong to take that money when I have these feelings for her; the sort that grip you softly around your every part.

I can't do both; move out immediately and also give Zasha her money back. Especially because Zasha paid a lot more for me than I actually got paid to romance her. But what if I do return what she paid, and then stop the sessions in the hope of getting to know each other in real life? Will she still want me? What if she just sees me as a merry gigolo, you know, a fun-time boy?

My head is pounding from my lack of sleep. Yawning, I get changed and scarper to work.

My workplace is eco-friendly, very green, some would even say too green. The CEO believes in planting a tree wherever you can. So if you go inside the building, you will see more trees than a forest. But even better than that, some idiot planted an invasive species in the soil by the reception desk. They thought it looked nice, so they brought a cutting when they returned from a trip to Japan. It turned out to be Japanese knotweed. Then, during the pandemic it ran amok, growing over walls, desks, computers. At some point next year we're going to have to move offices so that it can be dealt with. But for now, when I go to work I am surrounded by malevolent twigs. And that's just the people.

Getting to my desk – after sweeping aside the overhanging foliage- my colleague spins around, "Hey Jai, the big man wants a word with you."

The 'big man' being my boss Dave, who runs the different R&D teams.

"Can't mate, have the scrum meeting to get to, innit?" I retort.

"He looked serious, you should go. You can catch up with the team afterwards."

Hm. This will be fun.

Dragging myself to Dave's office I sigh loudly.

"Morning Jai," Dave says. Dave is from San Francisco, but moved to London to lead the English office, and because he's a British football nut.

"Morning. Watch last night's football? We crushed your shitty team."

I didn't watch the football. Usually I support Valley Green FC but

I had far better people to preoccupy myself with. Thoughts of pleasuring Zasha just hours ago flares a spark to my dick. Not appropriate in the boss's office.

"Yeah, one and only time mate. One and only time," I vaguely counter. Football banter doesn't need much.

I sit down and try and smile at Dave. Bet he's going to fire me.

"I guess you know your probation ends tomorrow right?" Dave casually dangles that sword of Damocles.

"Yeah, yeah was aware of that."

"Okay well, I have some news for you," he says slowly. Before making a steeple with his fingers and tapping his forefingers together like he's making a difficult decision.

I grip the arms of the chair. Fucker's going to do it, he's going to fire me.

"Been talking to the team; they tell me you're surly, you go to the pub at lunch, you're always dressed inappropriately, you overuse the coffee machine, you support a terrible football team, and you're a bit of a dick frankly."

What the fuck?

My heart hammers against my chest in panic.

"…and you'll fit right in. Congratulations Jai."

"You fucking bastard," I say to my boss, while technically being still on my probation. Wouldn't it be wank to be hired and fired on the same day?

Dave's lips spread into a wide grin.

"You're a great designer and developer Jai. Never met a guy who could knock the nail on the head with the visual element, the mechanics and the programming like you do. You're a…you're a triple threat! Keep this up, and next quarter you might just find yourself being promoted."

Okay, this is brilliant. Definitely can quit on Rent-A-Romance then. I'll soon be able to earn enough to extract myself from living with Nellie.

But can't quit on Zasha, don't want to quit on Zasha.

That's going to be a problem.

CHAPTER 11

Zasha

~Hockey Romance: A "You've got to choose" tale~

I can't skate. I mean, I was just sort of hoping it would be a pretend ice rink with pretend ice skating. Cannot think of anything less romantic than flopping all over the place on an actual ice rink. Trying not to break one's butt, or avoid getting fingers sliced off by errant skaters.

I make my way to Village Green tube station. It's between Wimbledon and Clapham Junction.

And the outfit. I mean, *What*?

It's a cheerleader outfit. I'm a grown woman, the skirt barely covers my intimates.

I almost didn't wear it but then I thought given the extortionate amount I've spent I might as well get into whatever Hamish is trying to achieve with this scenario. Hey, this is what I wanted… I think. Well not really.

I mean, when did you read a hockey romance where the female protagonist was a cheerleader? Like, never.

But Hamish knows what he is doing, right? Right.

I turn up to the ice rink and see it is full, and there seem to be a few people dressed in the ice hockey uniform of the Village Green Comets. Fast-paced music plays and a DJ grooves away to himself. The DJ's fashion taste is from the way back nineties; Spliffy jeans, a long ponytail and indoor sunglasses. This is going to be embarrassing.

Where is Jai? Late as usual? That's when I spot a man struggling to get into an ice hockey uniform while sitting on a bench next to the ice rink. Jai.

Jai is tumbling all over the place trying to yank on the ice hockey padding, which he is struggling with even though he is sitting on the bench.

But Hamish said they all skate like champs? I walk down the stairs towards the ice rink. I still need to hire my boots.

Just to let Jai know I am here, I walk over to greet him. Even while resembling an awkward marshmallow wrestling with himself he is sexy. His thick dark locks cascade over his face as he swears profusely. Pleasant sensations sparkle in my tummy and make my heart pitter patter.

I have spent the week in a daze of memory and fantasy. Jai's hands on my thighs, between my legs, touching, kissing, his hardness rubbing against my back. That warm breath on my ear.

We've been messaging this week, he always gets back to me pretty quickly and his messages are....sometimes sweet. Sometimes dirty. Just with a few quick texts I've laughed and lusted after this man.

And how I have lusted after Jai Minnox.

As if he is reading my scorching minxy thoughts Jai looks up at me directly and waves awkwardly.

I hear another familiar voice, "Zasha"...both Jai and I's heads whip around to see Magnus with two other faces that I recognise from the visit to the blues bar; a large handsome black guy and a Mediterranean man. Confusingly they are wearing ice hockey outfits too, and skating expertly. It's interesting, Jai seems so different from the other Romancers, but in a good way.

Magnus does a twizzle on the ice and skates over in a cocksure fashion, "Hey girl. How's it going? Not over playing romance with this loser yet?"

Jai looks pretty annoyed, "What you doing here Magnus?"

"Well, Kwame, Roman and I are *actually* on the ice hockey team. We don't need to play pretend," Magnus then does a totally needless but entertainingly nifty dance on the ice while fixing his gaze on me. I am guessing he's trying to rock my socks off. The funny thing is that to look at Magnus he is a stone-cold fox, but he is such a cock that it makes him gross. Why is he such a jerk?

I sigh, "It's not very intimate having you three plus Jai."

Jai snaps, "No it's not. Hands off, alright Magnus?" Jai attempts to get up. However he stumbles on his skates like a baby bird that has fallen out of its nest. His legs wobble and he has to grip the side just to stand. He must be hating this. It is sweet that he is willing to undertake something that he thinks sucks just for my entertainment.

"You just wave your hand as a white flag of surrender when you finally need me to scoop you up in my arms, and carry you out. Okay buddy?" Magnus says to Jai, his grin malevolent. He then skates off, interweaving with Roman and Kwame who then break into twirly dances before skating off extra fast. They are such smug skaters.

Hoping that some distance will cool things down I decide to go and get my skates, "Hey Jai, just going to hire out some boots. I'll be back in a second."

This time I decide I'm not removing the coat. It's just a bit too embarrassing cavorting about dressed as a cheerleader in public. I do however have the script in my pocket. So far Jai and I have avoided going through Hamish's cheesy scripts, but for the ice rink we're really out of our element. The script will help give this all an anchor.

I approach Jai, still not keen to brave the ice rink, "Hey Jai, can we do the script?"

"I've kind of got mine in the locker with my coat. But you can do your script if you want, and I'll ad lib?" Jai suggests.

Nodding I walk like a fawn towards the ice, the boots are constricting my feet, making them ache uncomfortably. I wish I'd given it some deeper thought when Hamish said this scenario was in an actual ice rink. I'm just glad that Jai is just as rubbish as I am at skating. It would be mortifying if he was any good.

The DJ plays Bonkers by Dizzee Rascal and yells, "Wooo! That's right ice rats, we're bonkers aaiight! Go mental, here we go!" he then bops around, jumping up and down like a pogo.

Not to state the obvious but the ice is slippery. It's pretty unnatural to do this. I mean, didn't people start ice skating to escape the peril of the ice, not loiter on it? Okay, maybe not. But I don't get it.

I cling onto the side and try to drag myself over to Jai who is wearing his ice hockey outfit. A kid who *can* ice skate glides over with an evil, impish expression and breaks stop in front of us, sending a spray of ice in our faces. Confused we both stumble, our skates intertangling. We manage to detangle them by artfully yanking our legs away from the whole sorry mess.

Magnus skates by, "Need help yet *ma Cherie*?" he drawls.

"No," I give him a warning look but he laughs and skates off at a million miles an hour.

I try and use one hand to get the script. My legs nearly give way. I read what I can, "Hey Patrick O'Mallet, you're looking awfully hot in this cold, cold ice rink. By the way sweet sugar, I love your mullet."

So bad. Nope again.

I scrunch the script in my pocket.

"Jai. This is terrible. Say, did your costume come with a mullet?"

there must be a twinkle in my eye. Jai wearing a mullet would make my day.

"Yeah, but you're not making me wear it Zasha."

The explicit version of Boom Boom Boom by The Outhere Brothers plays. The DJ is now going crazy, "Fucking Yeah! That's right. Class! Classic! Shake your arses you slags!"

Two ice stewards – one dressed as Santa's elf and the other as a snowman- look towards the DJ with cross expressions. Perhaps they are not loving his fruity language during the family-friendly hour of ten o'clock in the morning. They skate towards the DJ in unison.

Jai looks at me and cracks up, and I laugh heartily along with him, "This is stupid Zasha, isn't it? We're both having a rubbish time. Come on. Let's go get a slushie."

We edge towards an exit from the rink -our legs akimbo as we clutch the side- and climb out. I am so relieved.

A kid comes running up to Jai looking at his ice hockey uniform, his big eyes darting up and down, "Oh this is so cool! Do you play for the Village Green Comets? Can you sign my autograph?"

"I don't play for them no," Jai corrects the kid.

"Why you in hockey garms then?" the little boy looks most disappointed.

"Do you want an autograph or not?" Jai says way more sassily than he should, considering he is the furthest thing from an ice hockey player in the vicinity.

"Yeah, yeah alright. You famous or something?" says the boy.

"Or something. You got something to sign on?" the little boy nods quietly and retrieves from his pocket a scrap of paper and a little red crayon. Jai takes the paper and crayon and scrawls his signature. The little boy breaks out into a smile as if Jai was a bona fide celebrity.

Before we go into the ice rink café, I look back at the ice rink only to see the DJ being wrestled from his booth, and the snowman ice steward plugging his own iPhone into the speaker playing Christmas tunes. Looks like we're not the only ones having a rough day.

We grab a slushie, and getting high off the sugar and additives we talk quite a bit.

"Zasha, so when are you going to date me for real?" Jai says looking at me playfully. I can't tell if he's serious or not.

"When I can afford to. You don't come cheap Jai," I say in partial jest.

Jai breaks a faint smile but appears tense. Like he wants to say something. I slurp at the slushie in anticipation.

Leaning forward, his voice a low rumble - he purrs, "Are you wearing the cheerleader's outfit under that?"

I nod slurping. His gaze lowers to my lips wrapped around the straw, sucking enthusiastically. You don't have to be a psychoanalyst to discern his inner workings.

He leans in, "And what are you wearing under *that* Zasha?"

I blush. Underneath the cheerleader outfit, I'm wearing peach lacy lingerie fully in anticipation of removing them. The way he is gazing at me, I ponder whether he is wearing x-ray specs.

He then leans back and clears his throat, "You're a girl nerd aren't you?"

"Just 'nerd' will do," patriarchy, up yours.

"Alright. Well. Would you like to come and see a historic exhibition on computers? There's even a reconstruction of the Antikythera mechanism. What do you think?"

Wait, Jai is suggesting something that doesn't involve us getting jiggery pokery with each other? Now this is novel.

"Sure," I say as coolly as I humanly can. I don't know what the

Antikythera mechanism is, but clearly Jai thinks it's the sexiest thing since chocolate cruffins.

He smiles like he has won the lottery.

Look at us, we're not just doing smutty things; we're also having good clean fun.

Then Jai leans in – lips brushing my ear, "Then after that exhibition, I want to take you back to my office round the corner and christen my desk with you," I gasp before smiling, entirely agreeable to this notion.

Okay, now we're back to the familiar territory of having bad dirty fun. The thought of being spread and fucked on Jai's desk turns me up to eleven. I must have that written all over my face because his smile takes on a different characteristic, he stares at me as if I am hunting game.

"Zasha, what are you thinking girl?"

"I am thinking, that you are a terrible and delectable man Jai Maddox," with this, a sense of daring permeates and I rub my ankle along his calf under the table. He jerks in surprise and his eyes momentarily widen. No one is looking, but it feels risqué. My heart is racing.

Then he recomposes himself before chuckling, "Greedy Zasha, at it again. What, your slushie's not enough for you? Need something else to get your mouth around?" speaking in a low, dangerous rumble his hands grip the edge of the table.

Caressing my boot further up Jai's calf, I am careful to keep the blade of my skates tilted away.

I imagine he's hard by now. I hope that I'm driving him crazy.

He's driving me crazy.

Jai

I am going to take her so hard she will see stars. She's a bad tease, who knows exactly what she is doing to me.

Then I have an inspired thought.

I take her hand from across the table, "Come on Zasha, you're in for it now. I am going to take you to a very special place."

We return our skates, and holding hands -our fingers woven together- small sparks exchange between us. We saunter out of the ice rink; our destination is a few streets down. This idea is brilliant; in my horny, depraved mind it's what we both need.

"Where are you taking me Jai?" Zasha appraises me with an excited expression.

"Somewhere special, where I go to unwind."

We're nearly there, it's just around the corner.

We enter the Tantric Touch Adult Massage parlour.

Zasha grabs my sleeve with the other hand, her eyes look like they're going to pop out. Pulling me in she hisses, "Jai, you brought me to a…to a…sex den? I don't even know what this is. What kind of shady business is this?"

"The best kind of shady business. You'll like this," Although scoping around, there is no denying that this place has an air of the brothel about it. The ladies walking around in see-through lingerie do set a particular tone. Zasha is staring at them aghast. She then gazes at me dubiously and shakes her head. She is definitely judging me.

Now thinking about it, this might have been a horrible idea to come here, but if I back out now it will look like I am just a perv with something to hide. Which I am not. I am a perv with *nothing* to hide; well, apart from everything I have to hide; living situation with crazy ex, fake gigolo etcetera. Plus, I know exactly what I want to do with Zasha, and something tells me she'll like it.

Rumour has it that if you ask the parlour for the Vegas Special you get the room to yourself. It costs one hundred quid for thirty minutes. A mate told me it was well worth it; he brought an ex-girlfriend to the parlour once. Although maybe it's no coincidence that she became an ex-girlfriend shortly after.

Maybe this was a foolish idea.

Before I have a chance to grab Zasha's hand and tell her it was all a practical joke Miss Harbotham comes sauntering out and sees me, "Jai. What are you doing here?" she asks coquettishly.

Zasha looks at me searchingly.

"Uh hi Miss Harbotham. This is my lovely –"

Zasha shakes her head cautiously, like she doesn't want her real name revealed and associated with this fine establishment.

"-Girl, this is my lovely girl. Could we go for the Vegas Special? Thirty minutes?"

Miss Harbotham smiles approvingly, "Finally Jai, you visit us for our *raison d'etre*, rather than just to fanny around. Now excuse a girl a little upselling. You can buy a box of toys that you can also take home after the session. What do you say?"

"Yeah whack it on," Zasha is looking at me now as if I am the most suspect man in the world.

"Hm, Jai. What *are* you getting massaged when you come here?" Zasha's squinting at me now, as if she's trying to see into the murky depths of me.

Miss Harbotham smiles serenely, "Don't worry darling, Jai likes legit massages. He comes with his football team. They don't all have legit massages I can assure you. He's a good boy."

Miss Harbotham cracks open a door and looking at me drawls, "It has all been deep cleaned today. The box of toys is in the corner, all brand new. Enjoy."

Inside there is a white massage table covered with a white towel and rose petals strewn on top. Subtle. This must be the erotic massage parlour equivalent of the honeymoon suit. Sauntering over to the box of toys in the corner I crack it open, almost expecting it to dazzle with illuminating light. Inside the box there is massage oil, a boxed vibrator and a butt plug that looks like a heart-shaped jewel. In ordinary times, the cost of the toy box is extortionate for what you get, but when I have my beautiful Zasha to corrupt, every penny is worth it.

Zasha looks at me, "God *who are you* Jai?"

Turning around, I grin at her and cup each of her shoulders with my hands, "Zasha, Zasha, Zasha. I am the man who has spent the past week thinking about all the depraved things to do to you," I gaze at her beautiful face, until my eyes meet her plump lips. How am I to resist?

I bend my head down and kiss those lips. Cupping her face, my fingers brushing her cheeks. She sighs and relaxes into me as I kiss her.

"So the safe word is 'Sin Bin'…are you okay with that, would you be okay with me restraining you, perhaps spanking you my delicious Zasha?" I purr.

"Yes to all of the above," she says quietly.

"Good," I grunt.

My hands leave her face and I smack her lovely plump bottom, making her squeak and jump much to my satisfaction. Her bottom is so delectable that it's the sort made to be bitten, like good cake.

Then she comes to her senses, "Jai! I cannot believe you brought me to a brothel," Huh. I didn't think of Tantric Touch that way. Although technically I suppose it is; given you can hire an escort with the Seattle special; so-called because it leaves you sleepless. Yeah, and let's not forget the whole happy endings business.

Zasha bites her lower lip seductively, making my heart beat more violently before she pouts, "If my feet were not sore from the skating I would run away so far. I sweat Jai, I don't care how good you are at getting me off."

"Well, I think Zasha you haven't legged it because you're intrigued. Now let's take off your clothes. You're getting a very thorough sports massage."

I help Zasha to remove her coat. As I do I kiss the nape of her neck, pressing my hardness against her. I place the coat behind the door hook.

Dressed as a cheerleader in a red and white outfit that barely covers her bottom, she looks incredibly tempting.

"Give me a ra ra," I jest.

"Ra ra," she says meekly and pretends to punch the air with imaginary pom poms, making her tits bounce pleasingly. With both my hands I reach out and cup her tits, my thumbs circling her nipples through her top, those sensitive, perky nubs that belong between my teeth. Her eyes flutter to a close and she groans, arching her back towards me. Her body begging for more. I squeeze both her nipples and yank them towards me. Her groan lowers and it is almost as if the walls of her inhibitions are falling, just for me. I bet she is dripping between her thighs.

"Now there's a thought, you bouncing up and down all day long, just to cheer me on in performing," drawling huskily I playfully mock her. Sometimes I cannot help being a cheeky fuck.

As Zasha goes to whack me with the back of her hand for my smart mouth I grab her wrist and pull her in for a kiss. Her tits press against my chest and her soft lips make way for my tongue as I work it into her mouth, making it my own.

"God you don't look half as depraved as you are," Zasha breaks off the kiss to say breathlessly.

Chuckling I tuck a stray strand of her curly hair behind her ear, "I'll take that as a compliment. Now as sexy as this costume is, let's take this little number off shall we? I want you naked on that table," I plant a kiss before helping her to remove the cheerleader outfit, revealing a peach bra. I breathe in sharply at the sight of her voluptuous body in little but her lacey peach lingerie, she is so fucking sexy.

Leaning down I bite her nipples through the bra, Zasha gasps. Her eyes following me to see what diabolical thing I plan to do next. Chuckling mercilessly at her predicament I circle her until my chest is against her back, I trace my lips across the back of her shoulder as I unhook her bra, letting it fall to the floor. She breathes harder, harsher. Then, dropping to my knees I lift her skirt, clutching it against her belly while I tug her peach panties down with my teeth. The contrast between the peach and her dark, glossy skin is driving me insane. She whimpers sweetly as I inhale the heady scent of her aroused sex -the pink inner lips gleaming- and bury my nose into her glistening folds.

She is naked and vulnerable. I am clothed and rock-hard.

"On the table," I demand, my voice low and rough. Barely getting the words out I realise I have gone into caveman mode. I am trying hard to keep it together though, otherwise, there won't be much point in hiring this place out to massage Zasha.

Zasha walks over to the table, watching me with inquisitive eyes as she does so. She lingers, unsure of what to do next. I know *exactly* where I want her.

"Climb on, face down," I tell her. Zasha climbs onto the table as I approach, whimpering in anticipation, she shudders and so too does her perfect arse. I encircle her, prowling. What shall I do next to my naughty, horny girl?

Her round bottom is delicious marvel, I want to bite it, so I do. I bend down, and bite the soft flesh, enough to leave a little red imprint on my teeth without breaking skin.

"Oww! That's the opposite of a massage, Jai – what the hell?" her head cranes around to give me a good telling-off. However I don't feel bad, instead, I admire the little red mark left and rub it fondly on her delectable behind.

To add insult to injury I slap her bottom, "That Zasha is what happens when you have a bottom too beautiful to resist. I want to eat it."

Zasha moans and places her head back down on the table. I go to the box and pick up the oil.

Taking the oil I open the bottle and rub it between my hot hands. It smells like rose and sandalwood. Warming the oil in my hands I decide that I'm going to tease Zasha. I decide to start with her calves. Massaging slowly In little circles I travel up her shapely calves until I get to her thick thighs. Shiny slickness spreads across her dark skin as I rub my hands with increasing vigour across her supple physique, massaging every inch I can lay my hands upon.

"Part your thighs for me Zasha," she does, but rather than rub her inviting pussy, puffy from arousal and glistening wet, I rub the junction between her swollen pussy lips and thighs with both hands. She moans.

"Touch me, please," she begs shamelessly.

I smile, "Patience sweetheart," she moans, I can't tell if it's from arousal or exasperation. Probably both.

My hands travel up to her big, gorgeous bottom. I resist the urge to smack it again, and instead let my oiled hands glide up and squeeze both mounds, rotating them together with my grip. Zasha is moaning and panting away, her back rising and falling more dramatically as her arousal grows from my touch. Exploring her further, my hands glide up her back, to her shoulders and down her arms, rubbing my hands across her muscles, massaging as I traverse her body. Then I stop and walk back to the box to grab the vibrator.

"With a good massage, it's important to find the right pressure points. Relieve that tension. Get the circulation going. Wouldn't you agree?"

Cracking open the vibrator box I take out the pink rabbit vibrator and press the button. It starts to whirr to life, vibrating gently – the lowest setting.

"Yes, tension relief is most important," barely able to gasp out her words, she'll lose the power of speech entirely once I'm done with her.

"Good girl. Now show me that pretty face," Zasha turns her face to me so I can see the profile. Her eyes are trusting, lips parted from lust. I caress her jaw and run my thumb across her cheekbone. I've never wanted anybody more; I am rock hard for her. A lot of my thoughts are occupied with Zasha these days, it's fair to say I'm infatuated.

"Open your mouth," she does so, a little smile twitching at the corner of her lips.

With her mouth parted I rasp, "Stick your tongue out."

"Like this?" she asks, jutting out her little pink tongue, her eyes meet mine. The sight of her overwhelms me, just looking at her has my cock oozing seed.

I run my thumb across it, realising it hasn't tasted my cock yet, "My perfect, delicious slut, what a good girl you are."

I take the vibrator -mildly buzzing away- and place it on her eager tongue. She squeaks as it vibrates on her tongue and looks up at me questioningly. I rub the length of it across until it is nice and wet from her saliva.

"Suck," I say hoarsely. She closes her mouth around the vibrator, I nearly cum there and then, watching her lips oscillate as she swallows around it. Gently I push the vibrator in and out between her lips as she drools a little.

"Good Zasha, you suck things so prettily, my greedy girl. That's it, nice and wet," my cock is now so hard in my pants it is threatening to split them open. This is taking all of my willpower not to pounce on her and pummel my swollen shaft deep inside her.

I pull the vibrator out of her mouth with a pop before running it down the length of her back, and then using it to tap her thighs apart. She willingly spreads her legs open into a 'V' shape, casually slung both sides of the massage table. She rotates a foot in anticipation.

"Jai…" she whispers quietly. She probably wanted to say something cheeky but thought better of it. She certainly doesn't want me to stop.

I decide to tease my delicious Zasha, and run the vibrator along the lips of her pussy. The buzz mutes as it meets the sensitive folds, taking care to avoid the stiff peak of her clit - oscillating gently from the buzzing. She wiggles trying to angle it against her entrance now sticky with her cream, "Absolutely not greedy girl, always wanting to be stuffed."

I smack her bottom and she cries out.

"You're so mean," She hisses, her hands now clutching the side of the table needily.

The vibrator dawdles and then finally circles her engorged clit; poking out and eager. I cannot help it, I press the tip of the vibrator head against her clit and then hear Zasha moan, watching as her back arches.

"Jai, that's perfect yes," my greedy girl is expecting that I am going to let her cum just like that. Sadistically I take the vibrator away and then push just the tip into her wet core. She tries to push herself against it, but when she does I pull it out.

"No…you're being cruel," Zasha complains. Yeah, I am, and I'm enjoying it, playing her like a fine instrument. Her moans are my music.

"Well given you're into pirates, leather men and hockey players, I can safely say that you like your men mean," I enjoy taunting her, denying her the release that she seeks, but it is hard not going all the way. Making her cum screaming all around the vibrator would tip me over too, but it's worth depriving her to draw it out, bask in her sweet suffering. If only to watch her like this. I could watch her like this all day.

She protests, "Not into leather men."

I push the vibrator, still wet from her saliva, deep into her tightness. She clenches around it, and I see the vibrator jerk in my hands as she does.

"Oh yes," she moans as I slowly fuck her with it, wishing it was me. God, jealous of a vibrator; problems of the modern age. My cock is so hard it is nearly hurting.

I turn up the vibrator to its highest setting until Zasha is squealing continuously, trying to bounce against the toy, her oiled bottom quivering. The visual, *fuck*, it's going to be there for the rest of my life. It will be my go-to memory whenever I'm having a shitty day. Unable to resist, I spread the cheeks of her bottom and look at the tight pucker of her rosebud. I bet this is a girl who likes being filled in all her holes.

I shove the vibrator in her creaming entrance and leave it there as she gently humps against it, moaning louder and louder. Going to the box I fish out the jewel-shaped butt plug. It's very twinkly. Returning to the massage table and my enraptured Zasha I spread the plug against her sodden pussy to lubricate it. She shudders animalistically. Then parting her cheeks I work the butt plug into her tight rosebud.

Zasha arches her back, "Oh my god Jai!" her eyes roll back.

Grabbing her bun to keep her back tightly arched, tits in the air I whisper in her ear, "Do you like this Zasha, getting your holes filled? Well, there is one more hole, isn't there? A pretty neglected little bud of yours. That needs to be stretched too, make sure you're stuffed." I run my fingers over her mouth, her lips as she gazes at me, her eyes streaming with pleasure, and press my thumb into her mouth. She sucks it wantonly, her body now slick with sweat, oil, and her own cum.

This is my tipping point. Removing my thumb from her hot mouth I hurriedly remove my T-shirt and unzip my trousers and boxers, my straining cock springs to life, precum oozing from the crown. I place my thumb back into her mouth again, enjoying feeling her lap against it hungrily. Zasha sucks my thumb like it's a cock as the vibrator works within her. The way her hips are grinding the table the little rabbit ears are probably thrumming against her clit.

Wordlessly I withdraw my thumb from her lips, and then caressing the shaft of my cock I rub the precum along her lips, like a gloss. Would love to see her wear that to a party. Zasha smiles; and her tongue darts out, lapping up the cum. The texture of the flat of her tongue against the head of my crown is almost too much.

"*Fuckkk*, that's it, take me all in. Good girl. Suck," Groaning I weave my fingers into her thick afro hair. I push my shaft into her mouth, making her gag and swallow around the length of my diamond-hard cock. Her head bobs along my length trying to please me, as her brown-eyes lock onto my own. She is writhing now, all of her holes filled. My greedy girl. But then I see the vibrator work its way out, probably from her wet pussy gripping around it so tightly.

She doesn't stop, she keeps going as I fuck her face, enjoying her full lips wrapped around my length.

"God yes Zasha," I relish the feeling of her curly locks between my fingers, and as I look into her eyes I realise I cannot get enough of her. All of me feels like it is spilling over.

With that thought my balls tighten and I do one hard thrust within her mouth, making her gag. I feel myself cumming, hard, raw and uncontrollable. I want to cum on her face but Zasha works a hand at the base, almost as if she can read my thoughts and instead, I cum deep into her throat -in the warmth of her velvety mouth- and she drinks it all up, her throat working and lips tightening around my shaft. The thought of her drinking in my cum is nearly too much to bear. She is a dirty, bad girl and everything that I want.

Reluctantly, once I am fully spent, I withdraw. A little bit of cum is on the corner of her lips. I scoop it with my forefinger and then take advantage of her parted lips, work my finger in.

"All of it Zasha, every last drop."

Zasha

The sensation of being filled by Jai, overwhelmed by him in the best possible way; carries me to new heights. My body feels ablaze, as if it were turning into light and fracturing into rainbows. I was so, so close to coming, but then the vibrator within me slipped out. I feel so frustrated and aroused that my fingers claw at the table, even as I continue to swallow Jai's come down my throat.

Jai is still caressing my jaw and looking down at me with a particular intensity, his face blank and jaw ticking. He is mesmerised and dazed; caught in thought.

"I want to taste you Zasha, I can smell your sex and I want it on my tongue," his voice is low and dangerous; a predator readying for ambush.

Jai walks over, his feet a gentle patter as he works the vibrator out. But then he brings it round to my face. The pink vibrator is dripping with me. He made me this way.

"We said we were going to fill all of your holes, weren't we? Now open up," he caresses my jaw lightly with his long fingers.

"But it's still buzzing," I say in confusion.

"Yeah, now open up and don't drop it, otherwise I'll stop and smack your bottom," reluctantly I open my mouth as he places the buzzing vibrator between my lips. I taste myself as it brushes the back of my throat and buzzes. Sucking it in, the buzz reverberates down my tongue…my throat.

Jai walks back over but while I can hear him I don't see him. Suddenly I feel his oiled hands on my ankles, spreading apart my legs, exposing my swollen core -coated in my essence- to him. He drags my legs to the edge of the massage table.

Something presses between my legs and I can feel his hot breath against my cunt. Jumping in surprise at the sudden pleasant sensation, I feel a hard cold nub against my clit and I swallow around the vibrating pink plastic shaft in my mouth. His hands are now gripping my thighs, keeping them pinned apart; he burrows his nose in and I writhe gripping the table harder.

"God your scent, I could wear it. Remind myself of you day-in, day-out," then his tongue laps at my clit with fervour as if it were his last meal. I moan around the vibrator. I am so close to coming. The pressure is building, I can nearly feel it.

Jai's hands leave my spread thighs and I feel him manipulate the butt plug, softly pushing it in and out in short, punchy strokes, just as his other hand works one finger, then two, and then finally a third within cunt, stretching my drenched walls. Desperate, I jerkily hump back as he stokes up a blaze between my thighs, while the vibrator relentlessly oscillates in my mouth. My eyes stream with tears from the sensory overload.

His three fingers -stretching me- curl within my core, massaging my G-spot, I groan. All the while his tongue assaults my clit as his other hand uses the butt plug to pummel my bottom.

Soon I clamp down hard on his fingers, hard around the butt plug. I squeal around the vibrator as the orgasm crashes through my body like a hurricane, ripping me apart -ripping everything apart- in cascading waves of sheer ecstasy and spreading a glowing, pulsating warmth from my core that doesn't stop, but takes me to new heights. But Jai doesn't stop, he keeps going until I open my mouth and let the vibrator slip out. Moaning so loud I don't care if everyone can hear me. Moaning so loud that the street outside can probably hear me.

"Jai, oh my god," I shudder.

Being the shameless villain that he is, he lightly chuckles at my predicament, before slowing down, but he doesn't take the butt plug out, instead he pushes it deeper in, almost screwing it. I shudder and twitch, my body a mass of sensitised, excited nerves. He's not finished with me yet.

I feel his hands around my waist and then he flips me over so I am looking up and can see him. His eyes have a dark fire within, like he's possessed. His cock is back to straining upwards, bopping along.

"Zasha, Zasha…if I fuck you on this table, are you going to be able to control yourself? Can't have you creaming too soon around my cock, like the insatiable girl that you are," Jai's mocks playfully. He crawls over me on the white massage table and grasps my breasts, kissing one and then the other, before biting each nipple. My thoughts are jumbled and all I can focus on is the pulsating pleasure enveloping me…Jai enveloping me.

Jai saunters over to his trousers and finding a condom, rips it open and rolls it onto his swollen cock.

Soon Jai's face is flush with mine, he is right above me, his legs straddling my torso. He is using his elbows to prop himself up. I am pinned underneath him.

"I want to look at you Zasha, and I don't want you to close your eyes, do you understand?"

"Yes," I hiss, feeling his hardness pressed against my mons. He lifts one of my legs and wraps it around his back; my heel finds the small of his back.

Smiling Jai kisses my lips and then grabbing his shaft, guides the thick head of his cock within my dripping core, still fluttering following the aftershocks of my climax.

As he enters me his body presses against my own, and his lips caress mine as our eyes make contact. My eyelids flutter from being overly sensitised as he rocks within my wet core, stretching my walls, filling me up. The strokes of his cock within me are slow and hard. Jai's tongue slides within my mouth, against my own tongue. The rhythm of his aggressive kiss and the hard strokes of his cock in my cunt meet, a dizzying dance of being possessed by Jai Maddox. That is not all, the butt plug is still planted firmly within me and as I rock my hips up to meet his own and grind against him, I feel it bury itself into my bud, increasing the sensation of being stretched by Jai's shaft.

Jai whispers into my ear, "Beautiful Zasha, I could do this with you all day, all night and never stop. I could get lost in you and forget myself," his voice crackles with urgency. He means it. I look at him mesmerised. It is hard to find the words, but heaven would be fucking Jai endlessly, for all of eternity.

Jai cups my chin between thumb and forefinger and forces me to look at him, "I am yours Zasha, if you'll have me. Will you be mine, be my girl?" His dark hair is cascading forward, brushing my cheek. His eyes are pitch black.

When I don't say anything, trying to understand the question his hips rock against my own even more fervently. I can feel the dam swell as my pussy clenches around him, trying to grasp his cock.

He repeats the question, "Will you be mine?"

As the climax mounts, my body melting around him even as my core tightens itself around him I say quietly, "Yes."

He growls and then picks up the pace in a brutal frenzy, his hip bone crashing against mine, his chest rubbing my nipples, I feel the butt plug bury even deeper and my pussy clenches hard, spasming around his thick girth and soon I come all around him, trying to pull him in within my depth and keep him with me. Drowning in sweet torment I wish for him to join me as I ride this bliss he has gifted me with.

Jai kisses me hard, deep, his tongue forcing mine flat, dominating me.

Then I feel him swell gently within as he fills his condom with his seed. Our breath is heavy, our limbs are entangled. His gaze burrows into my own, fusing us together.

Neither of us say anything, but he is looking at me like a man who was lost in the desert, and has finally found his cool water.

Afterwards we are both shuddering, wet, twitching. He continues to kiss me deeply as if he were melding with me.

We could do this all day, we could –

A brutish knock on the door reminds us we're not even going by the hour, "Hey, thirty minutes! We're not running a charity here for horny nerds! You have five minutes!"

"Sorry Miss Harbotham. We'll be out soon," Jai shouts back aggrieved.

I look at Jai, almost feeling too shy to talk to him.

I also have a butt plug still buried in me which I will need to remove.

There is a hammering at the door, "If you're in for another two minutes I am charging you one thousand pounds." Miss Harbotham bellows.

"That's ridiculous!" Jai shouts back in umbrage.

We hurry into our clothes and place all the sex toys in the zip compartment of my bag. Miss Harbotham has pursed lips as we emerge from the room. She looks displeased.

"I don't like to have my time wasted. We have a Seattle special in less than an hour. Your DNA won't remove itself. Get out so we can clean."

I head to the bathroom and remove the plug, cleaning it before also placing it along with my horde of sex toys, stowed away in my large bag.

We walk out, Jai grabs my hand and gazing down, he grins. His eyes dance with joy, with mischief. His smile is so contagious that I smile back, squeezing his hand. I still feel the aftershocks of the orgasm thrum through my being. It feels like they will never leave. From now onwards, I shall just float around on an orgasmic cloud, using it to glide above London like a magic carpet. Free transport and endless orgasms; I'll put those on my

Christmas list.

Out of the massage parlour I get the distinct feeling someone is looking at me, and it isn't Jai. I glance straight ahead and immediately see that across the busy road there is a woman in a brown trench coat and hat watching us, scowling.

"Jai, do you see that woman watching us?" I tug his hand to get his attention.

"Nellie," He whispers, a worried expression etched upon his features.

"Nellie?" What *isn't* he telling me?

He clears his throat, "No one. That's what I said. No one."

That's *not* what he said, but okay. I drop it, and all the while I get a sense of unease, and it's not from having had a plug up my butt.

A bus passes and the woman mysteriously disappears.

"She's gone Jake, how did she disappear like that? One minute she's there…and the next she is not," I whisper my voice barely a crackle.

"She must have got on the bus. Come on, let's go out, I want more Zasha time if I may," his voice sounds tense though. This boy is not telling me everything.

CHAPTER 12

Jai

That *was* Nellie. The way she stared at us. Dead creepy. Why was she there? Has she been…following me?

It sets me on edge. Something tells me Nellie isn't going to let this one lie.

I turn my focus onto Zasha. Lovely Zasha, beautiful Zasha, Zasha I can't keep my mind off. And now, she's agreed to go out with me, although I did have her pinned underneath me when I asked her. Well, never mind the method, it's the result that counts. I couldn't be happier. Floating on cloud nine.

Yeah but, you have to tell her about Nellie. That fucker speaking is my conscious. Of course I am going to tell Zasha about Nellie, the ex-girlfriend who I am tied up in a mortgage with. Just not right now. No, not today; the day when Zasha and I have finally hooked up.

There are little stalls that look like Christmas cottages curled within an area of South Bank, festoon lights connect them like a glittering web in the late afternoon. People bustle but the atmosphere is festive, a gentle spirit of togetherness permeates the air. Adjacent to the stalls this year is a giant yurt with a silent mime performance taking place called "Mark in the Dark." I've been reading all about it, apparently it's very avant-garde, profound. I resolve to take Zasha, not just because it's a good opportunity to grope her with the lights off. It will feel like our first proper date, a bit like going to the theatre. Looking at the times on the phone, there is a showing in twenty minutes.

"It's strange," Zasha says, "I've lived in London all of my life and never come to the Winter market."

"That's bananas Zasha, where do you go?" we're waiting at a stall for our mulled wine and free mince pie.

"Usually we're back in Barbados as a family for Christmas, my folks live out there now, my Dad has a jazz joint by the beach. But this year I had too much work and I couldn't get the cover," Zasha sounds a little sad. I squeeze her hand.

This market is something special to me, "I come every year. Wouldn't miss it, not even for a holiday in the sun. Unless of course, I got to watch you on the beach," smiling ruefully we get to the front of the queue. I imagine Zasha on a Barbados beach in a scanty barely-there bikini, cavorting while throwing hot glances over her shoulder at me with come hither eyes. Now that would be a reason to miss the winter market.

"You come here every year, why every year?" she asks as we get closer to the front of the queue.

A sadness creeps into my chest, like a part of myself is missing and I just need to fill it, "It brings back memories of my mam, she passed when I was twelve. She used to bring me and my siblings here. We'd have a hot chocolate, candied nuts and mince pie. She'd always have mulled wine. The scent of mulled wine reminds me of her."

Zasha gazes at me, her eyes brimming, "I'm sorry Jai."

I shrug, "It's okay." Before the sinking feeling starts to dig in and the tears breach, a guy with a very long moustache and top hat serving the mulled wine takes my order. I glance down, Zasha's still looking at me, searching me, searching *into* me.

The guy serving the mulled wine clears his throat, "And now what may I get you, my delightful connoisseurs?"

"Mulled wine please," Zasha asks politely, her hands propped on the stall.

"Well, will that be mulled wine with cloves steamed with the essence of orange peel, or mulled wine with a dash of masala and a hint of birch sap?" the man asks, his eyes popping wide with enthusiasm.

"Nah, just mulled wine please," I say. The original stuff is best.

The man looks aghast, "We don't do. Just. Mulled. Wine. We're artisanal mulled wine innovators who are bringing to you the latest flavour edits."

This guy is starting to piss me off, but I don't want to ruin this for Zasha, "Mulled wine with cloves."

"Ah I think what you mean to say young man is mulled wine with cloves, steamed, with the essence of orange peel," he says somewhat smugly, a smirk making his moustache seemingly curl upwards, like a facial hair erection.

Inhaling and exhaling deeply I crick my neck, "Yes. That must be it," I respond through gritted teeth.

The dickhead continues, "The orange peel essence was imported from the heady, Mediterranean climes of Valencia, a rather unique place in *Espania* where the sun kisses the earth like a cherished lover whose body stretches over the land, breasts to the sky, thighs wide apart, opening themselves up to the sea." he stares at Zasha hungrily. The dirty bugger.

"Just give us both the mulled wine. Alright?" I snap impatiently. The man chuckles heartily and then like a dandy version of Salt Bae proceeds to sprinkle cloves into the mulled wine from on high, causing little bits of scalding splatter. A hot splash gets Zasha below the eye.

"Oww!" She cries, instinctively clutching her cheek and turning away from the stall.

"Fucking wanker," I say about the man under my breath. I check

Zasha's cheek, tipping her face up at me, "Are you alright love?"

"Yes," she says. Her pupils are heavily dilated, cheeks flushed. Then I remember the fact I made her cum for me only a short while ago. I wonder if she is craving me, just as much as I crave her.

I clear my throat, "I'll grab the mulled wine, and mince pies," shooting the man at the bar a dirty look I grab the mulled wine and accompanying free mince pie. He doesn't care, he's off torturing other seekers of festive beverages.

I wrap my arm possessively around Zasha's shoulders. We walk towards the tent showing Mark in the Dark.

Zasha

It feels good to have Jai's arm casually slung around my shoulder. To feel his warmth, the sensation, the heat, of Jai's body pressed against my own.

Jai's eyes sometimes dart to my body, coarsely assessing it, his fierce gaze then meets mine, stirring a light elation and dark desire. I am in trouble with this boy, I can't control the beating of my heart around him.

We go into the tent for 'Mark in the Dark', and Jai guides me towards the seating at the back. We sit as others do and I place my large bag on my lap. I am always so worried about losing it.

Jai grabs my hand.

This play has been described as heartwarming, profound and life-changing. I cannot wait to experience it.

I lean over to Jai, "So excited for this."

He brushes his thumb across the heart of my palm, "I bet you're excited. Tell me, are you as excited as you were in the massage parlour?" my cheeks heat up.

"Not quite as excited as that, no," I mutter.

Jai has an evil twinkle in his eye and he smirks. Conscious that others are taking their seats around me I say nothing and shoot him a warning look, as a flutter courses through to my very core. I want to drag him to the stage and mount him.

He chuckles, "Wordless are we Zasha? Strange that, if I recall you like putting your tongue to good use," my breathing hitches and I become hyper-aware of my surroundings as my arousal is reinvigorated, causing me to feel very self-aware.

He squeezes my hand. I squeeze back, my other hand on my bag, clutching it tightly.

Then thankfully the play starts. On the darkened stage a man comes out dressed in black. I guess that is Mark. He then starts miming away. Is there no speaking as part of this play? Hmm.

I try to get into it, but firstly it is hard to see the stage because it is so dark, and also without any spoken parts, one can only ponder what this is all about. I reposition the bag on my lap.

BUZZZZZZZ! The sound starts suddenly, and it's coming from my bag. It must be the vibrator. I must have turned it on by clutching the bag.

People turn around to look at me.

Then Mark the mime stops and bellows, "Whose phone is that? Turn it off! Bloody plebs."

I try and turn it off by groping the bag in desperation, but that doesn't work. I can't pull it out of the zip compartment and turn it off because then everyone will see I have a vibrator in my bag.

Someone taps my shoulder from behind, "I believe that's coming from your bag. You might want to turn that off."

Through gritted teeth I respond, "I am well aware, thank you very much."

A man yells at me, "Boo! Down with culture vandals!"

Before there is a mutiny and we're chucked out of the tent anyway, Jai grabs my hand and we totter out, my bag still buzzing away.

Once we are outside, Jai laughs incredulously, "That was brilliant. Ah Zasha, never a dull moment with you."

I whack him with my still vibrating handbag and then unzipping it slightly reach in and press the power button on the vibrator.

I stare at Jai crankily, wishing to salvage the last of my respectability – still riled from my public embarrassment, "I'm going home."

"I'm coming with you." He says without missing a beat.

We take the tube, and all the while, his finger circles and flickers my palm as if he were mimicking pleasuring me.

I lean in, "Jai, you're making me uncomfortable."

"Good," He whispers.

We take the underground tube to my place which is a fifteen-minute walk away.

Walking down a quiet suburban street, we pass two small shops which are closed for the night. Nestled between them is a deep alley. Jai pulls me into a darkened alleyway, his mouth immediately onto mine, his hand at my waist, squeezing it. He is hard. Again.

Breathlessly I say, "We can do this at my home."

"Yeah, but then we'd need to wait another five minutes, and I am just so turned on for you today. That's what happens when I see you only once a week," he moans into my ear.

"Oh God Jai, you tasty, yummy sex demon," I mumble near-incoherently as his hands roam my body.

He nudges my skirt and panties down and then with my derriere exposed he falls to his knees and flings my leg over his shoulder as I stand pressed against the wall. This is a man who loves to taste me, and well, I love him tasting me. Appreciation could not be more mutual.

Jai's mouth kisses the whole of my core, like a French kiss, before his tongue dips into my entrance, causing me to squirm against his sure grip. One of his hands idly plays with my swollen clit while the other mauls my bottom, grabbing it tight and pulling me further into his mouth.

His tongue laps away writhing, pleasuring me. Mmm, Jai's got a long tongue. The sensation of overworked clit being plucked once more sends me down a spiral where I am vulnerable to being pleasured, to climaxing easy for this man. Soon I feel myself clench down around his tongue, then as he flicks my clit one more time with his calloused fingers I clamp down, tripping into an orgasm, gushing my arousal onto his tongue. He murmurs approvingly. I have never had sex in public before; the thought reddens my cheeks. Jai is officially turning me into a hussy.

"Mmm good girl, we'll need to make a habit of that, I love your taste. Now turn around." he murmurs seductively.

I turn to face the wall, "What are you – " suddenly I feel his cock enter me hard and to the hilt, it is easy for him to do so because I am so aroused and drenched for him.

His hand finds my throat and grips it. Panting I pick up the pace – smacking my bottom against his hips, desperate for more of him.

"Do you like this Zasha? All your cream in your pussy makes it so easy to ride you however I want, wherever I want."

His filthy words make my eyes roll. The pleasure wells like a storm, threatening to take me down and turn me into a puddle.

I clamp down again, coming hard – the relentless orgasms almost feeling like an exquisite bruise deep within. I gasp for air as pure pleasure rolls over me. Jai, sensing my orgasm, picks up the pace, setting me aflame. As the feeling subsides he slows down, kissing my neck and jaw tenderly, "I'm sorry Zasha, I can't resist doing bad things to you, especially now that you're mine."

Jai rocks against my spent body, his cock still pummelling me. Soon his body tenses and I feel him expand within, and he comes, hard, his body stiffening.

God I must look preposterous in my cheerleader outfit.

Together we still ourselves, and then Jai turns me around, and crushes his mouth against my own, kissing me so deeply it sucks the air out of me. His hand skirts around and he cups my bottom and squeezes it with one hand while intertwining his fingers in my hair with the other. I feel totally, utterly possessed by him. Dazed almost.

Finally, Jai breaks off the kiss, his long fringe obscuring his gaze.

"Are you tired Zasha? I'm tired," Capturing his breath Jai tucks himself back into his trousers and zips up. I flip down my dress and pull up my knickers and tights.

"A bit, but it's only four o' clock," Suddenly I feel a bit like a girl who has had sex down an alleyway in the daytime…with a man she is technically paying for company.

I shuffle my feet insecurely at this thought. Jai studies me for a moment with a serious expression. Perhaps sensing my reticence he then picks me up and flings me over his shoulder, "Aah! Jai, warn me first!" I yell as my world turns upside down.

"Where would be the fun in that?" he responds cheerily as he traipses down the street.

Jai carries me to my home and only sets me down so I can open up the front door.

When I get back Phyllis is there, sitting in the living room in her pink Victorian bustle outfit resplendent with a bonnet encapsulating her afro, drinking her afternoon tea and nibbling a scone. She has her lacey pink parasol set behind her. Phyllis has a matching parasol for each outfit, and she has many outfits.

Phyllis raises an eyebrow to Jai, "One has male company for the evening I take it?" Phyllis talks in a mish-mash of ye olde words. I am never entirely sure if she is making fun, or if she truly believes herself to be a relic of the past.

I clear my throat, "Hey Phyllis, this is Jai, just going to grab a shower and yeah, if it's okay, he'll be staying with us….for the night."

Jai waves by flicking his wrist casually, "Lovely to meet you Phyllis."

"One welcomes you into this abode, however, *this* lady shall keep a wary gaze upon you should you have ill designs upon my dear living companion," Jai looks confused. I gently roll my eyes.

"Nice to see you Phyllis, enjoy your scone. Hope that's not all you're having for dinner," Phyllis eats like a bird, in part because she drinks an inordinate amount of tea.

"Only one of you in the bathroom at a time please. It is only proper. No debauchery in the latrine!" Phyllis bellows in a particularly unladylike way, as if reading my thoughts. I love Phyllis, but she is living her dream intensely. That also means preserving other people's chastity.

Going into my room we giggle and bolt the door.

Jai looks at me cheekily, "Do you think she'll let me take your virginity if I ask her for your hand?"

"Depends what you're planning to do with my hand," I respond coyly removing my coat and then unpeel my cheerleader outfit.

I walk up to Jai who is still clothed, "Jai, I'm going to have a shower and then come and cuddle you. Okay?"

He bends over and kisses my forehead then my lips, "Uh huh."

I have a steaming hot shower, washing the come, grime and dirt off. I potter back to my bedroom with a large white towel wrapped around me.

I am looking forward to a night of hotness with Jai. This is going to be non-stop. There will be so many orgasms my room will combust. This is going to be –

Jai is fast-asleep naked on the bed – evidently of like mind where the night would take us as he is spread like a starfish and snoring. I mean, it's been a tough day for him.

Chuckling I place on my nightie and then approach the bed. It's a chilly night and I don't want the lovely Jai to catch a cold, so I wrap the duvet around him, like a burrito. This means no bedding for me. Instead I grab a bunch of blankets that I keep strewn on top of an armchair in the corner of my room and then try and get comfortable underneath. But I can't, I'm shivering. It's probably a bit extreme. I should just wake Jai up but he looks so deep in slumber that I don't want to disturb him.

During the night I am woken by the sensation of a duvet settling over me and the warmth of Jai sliding in by my side, gently curling in next to me.

He slings his arm over my waist and whispers, "It's cute of you to wrap me up like a street food snack, but we need to warm you up."

Jai presses his chest against my back, his heart thumping like a gentle drumbeat against my skin. and caresses my tummy while throwing one of his long legs over my thigh, spooning me.

His electricity at my back at first awakens my senses, and then with the comfort of knowing he is there, it lulls me to sleep.

I drift off, wrapped in a warm blanket of Jai.

When I wake I feel Jai's hand still slung around my waist, his breath against my ear. I grasp my side table for my mobile. Jai murmurs with his low, seductive voice, "Morning, god I could get used to this."

He's a mind reader.

"Morning Jai, do you know you have morning wood?" I say, pressing my bottom against his hardness hopefully.

He laughs, "Why yes, I do…but I want to keep something back for when I see you later tonight. In the meantime, let's just embrace, like this." He presses against me, his arms wrapped around my waist.

Jai nuzzles my neck, "did you mean what you said yesterday, that you would go out with me? You would be mine?"

With his large hand splayed against my belly, he draws me closer into his embrace. I brush his fingers with mine as if they were candles and my fingers matches.

"Yes, although you did rather choose your moment." I recall that at the time, he had me pinned down in a delightfully compromising position. My state of mind could not have been more lust-drunk then, nor now.

"Yes I did…choose the moment," he purrs. Then slowly, teasingly he kisses the back of my neck, making me shiver with anticipation for this man.

If I could freeze a moment and live in it, it would be this one.

Eventually we both have to go to work. We kiss goodbye, but Jai promises to come round.

I look forward to it.

CHAPTER 13

Jai

Rocking up to work in yesterday's bedraggled clothes doesn't leave a great impression. But still riding high from my time spent with Zasha, I feel like I am dressed like a king.

Dave approaches and places his palms on my desk, leaning in, "Jai, you look like you've been dragged backwards into a hedge… or into the lap of a beautiful woman."

"Surely you mean it the other way around? She has been dragged into my lap."

Dave smiles like a proper wrong one, "Nah, that's just sexist. Look, Jai. Great, but…bring spares to work? Sunil over there practically lives in the office, he has like a wardrobe in the bottom drawer. Chantelle has a sleeping bag under her desk, but also a suit. Do something like that, aight?"

Sullenly, I nod at Dave. Man, it would be too depressing to find yourself living in the office. Thank God I'm not one of those desperados.

That evening I visit the Rent-A-Romance office for the team meeting. Every once in a while I catch myself grinning away, thinking of Zasha, sexy Zasha, sweet Zasha. I recall my hands against the curves of her body, her rich dark skin contrasting my own, her innocence, her naughtiness…I can't remember the last time I felt so hooked on anyone.

Stepping inside the office ten minutes late, the room goes quiet. This time Hamish is there with the guys. He stares at me solemnly.

"Hey Jai, good of you to join. You're late," says Hamish who is usually the tardiest of us all.

"Yeah, sorry about that. Had to go back home," mumbling, I plant myself on a sofa next to Kwame.

Hamish leans back and grimaces at me, "So we've just been talking. The guys over here are telling me you've been getting particularly lovey-dovey with your client."

Magnus interjects with more helpful information, "The clients are so vulnerable, you know? We're all just a little worried that Jai may be -how would you say?- *influencing* Zasha."

Gnashing my teeth I have a go at him, "It sounds like what you're worried about Magnus is that I am making my client happy, while your last one took one look at you and legged it."

Magnus leans forward, "Now look here-"

Hamish interjects, "Okay fellas, let's call it quits. You can go now. Except you Jai."

As everyone races out of the door, Magnus cocks his head over his shoulder before he leaves, "If you're not being improper with Zasha, then tell Zasha to call me for a *real* date. Cannot be too hard, if you two are just client and Romancer."

I reach up to grab Magnus by the scruff when he darts out. I sit back down and curse under my breath.

Now it is just me and Hamish. Hamish looks me up and down warily. He pulls out something from his desk. It resembles a photo album, "Do you know what this is Jai?"

"No," But I'm intrigued.

Hamish sighs fondly, his ashen fingers brushing the cover of the album, "Memories, memories of love, memories of romance. Guess who the first Rent-A-Romance Romancer was?"

"Who?"

There is a twinkle in Hamish's eyes, "Me. Come take a look."

I walk over to Hamish's desk. The photo album is open on a page with lots of monochrome photos from Hamish's youth. Most of them are of when he was a young, handsome rockabilly straddling his motorbike and gazing broodily at the distance with a cigarette hanging off his lip. There is something familiar about the young man in the photos, perhaps because it epitomises an era.

Hamish looks fondly at the photos, "When I was young I had so many adventures. Women went ga-ga me. There wasn't enough to go around. You know what I am saying?"

Don't even want to ask.

Hamish continues wistfully, "Those were the good old days. The glory days. After the war a lot of women had lost husbands, boyfriends, fiancés. Horny, lonely women. There I was, just a young buck around town. And guess what? I saw a gap in the market and I took it."

"So you became a gigolo basically."

Hamish looks at me as if I have flung him the deepest insult, "*No* I did not. I was something more profound...a fantasy, a dream, a lover. Take a look at that young man in the photo, that right there is a whole lotta man for a whole lot of women."

We both look at the photos for a few seconds in silence. Then I squint at it. I know why it's familiar.

"That's not you, that's James *sodding* Dean!" I shout.

"Whatever, potatoes, patatas. You hear what I am saying? I was just as magnetic," he slams the photo album shut.

"Why aren't there photos of you then?"

"Photography wasn't around when I was young, okay? Don't be a schmuck about it," squinting my eyes in disbelief I wonder what he is trying to say with all of this.

"Look, the real point I am trying to make is that I get it. I do Jai. All my baby mamas were clients of mine at some point or another. Magnus's mom was a Swedish model who just wanted to get a taste of Mr Dreamboat himself. Me. But son, this is my company. I'm gonna be throwing my hat in for mayor, so all I ask of you is keep your hose in your pants. Okay?" Hamish gazes at me with particular intensity.

The ship has sailed, but I nod all the same.

"Good. You're a good boy. You'll go far. Well that's it, that's all I had to say. Let's go home," Hamish slaps his hand on my back. He then locks up the office, however, as he's walking towards his car I exaggeratedly pat my jacket.

"Oh no! Looks like I forgot my wallet. Can I get the keys to go back in and get it?" I ask, trying to sound as authentic as possible.

"Sure, sure. Here you go kid," Hamish gives me the keys. I run to the cabin and when I get in I go straight to Hamish's desk. Opening his drawers I rifle through the filing cabinet. Thankfully Hamish is allergic to technology, making what I am about to do much easier. I find Zasha's file and then seeking out her bank details tap them down on my mobile.

I hear Hamish approach, the office door creaks open, "Everything okay there son?"

"Yeah yup, it fell under the desk. Now done," finishing my underhanded task I close the drawer just as he comes in, and misses the nefarious activity I am up to.

Hamish looks at me curiously, "Okay, uh. So let's go then."

Zasha

It's evening time and I am curled up in bed reading a smutty romance book, wrapped in my furry red nightgown while my hair is swaddled in a towel as my hot oil treatment works its magic. Jai has said he's coming back, but he'll probably be here closer to midnight given that it's already late. Because Jai enjoyed my spectacles last time, I have my saucy pink reading glasses on, as opposed to my other reading glasses which being tortoise shell, are not as provocative a colour palette.

If Jai's visiting late then I am going to be so tired for work tomorrow, because I am hoping for more than a snuggle from him. I've been thirsting for him all day; there were points today when I was deep in the coding, only to forget my line of thought while recalling our rather delightful dalliance together. Ah, the runtime loop of the heart.

I hear my phone buzz. Oh, a notification from my bank app. Here we go. Pain and torture. Let's just say my Rent-A-Romance subscription is not exactly a savvy money move, yes I have my early inheritance from my grandpa, but as per Jai's suggestion after I bought my games console to try out Starfield, my money is ever diminishing. I grimace. Opening the app the first thing I notice is the text in green, showing that I've been paid.

Strange.

The next thing I see is the amount; *five thousand pounds*!? That's the exact amount I paid Rent-A-Romance.

Hmm.

The payment reference on the screen makes me smile so much it hurts.

REF: YOU'RE GORGEOUS

It's from Jai, surely? Unless this is Hamish's foolish attempt to crack on to me. But what? But *how?*

My heart beats rapidly in elation. This must mean this is serious for him. I am *not* just a gig.

Just as I am getting excited, I hear a knock on my bedroom door. Walking over, I carefully balance my head-wrap with one hand so that it doesn't fall off.

Opening the door I see it is Phyllis, dressed in a cornflour-blue silk gown.

"Greetings good lady. How art thou?" Phyllis bows at me as if she were a lady-in-waiting. It's all a bit much, but that's Phyllis.

And equally, if there is anyone I can be a bit much around, it is my housemate, "Oh Phyllis, I think I am in love!" Clutching my hands to my chest, I let all the feels hang out. I'd feel stupid saying this in front of anyone else, including the Awkward Squad…perhaps especially the Awkward Squad.

"Not I hope, with that *knave*," narrowing her eyes she spits out her words like venom.

"Why Phyllis? You barely know him," surprised by her aversion I wonder if she sees something askew about Jai that I am missing…it does feel like he is holding something back. That woman standing across the road for instance when we went to the ice rink…but I also believe that he is genuinely into me. I wonder what her instincts are.

Well, I don't need to wonder, Phyllis is keen to tell me.

"I know devilish rakes such as he, tiresome fellows that are best refrained from," Phyllis sniffs. That's a dark warning.

Tilting my head I try my best to read her. Phyllis and I have shared our flat for a few years. This isn't just about Jai.

"Unpack for me please Phyllis, what is this really about?" sometimes you need to be direct with Phyllis. Otherwise it can be like the conversational equivalent of the ballroom dance from hell, which would probably actually be Phyllis's idea of heaven.

"Just, don't move out to be with him, okay?" Phyllis says in a quiet, vulnerable drawl. I feel a pang of guilt because honestly, it hadn't occurred to me before Phyllis said it, but the idea of living with the insatiable Jai Maddox is not unappealing. But I wouldn't want to abandon Phyllis as a housemate; we've had some good times. Terrible times too, like when we fell out over the curtain tassel knots now nailed to the wall, which she put up when I was on holiday in Barbados. Phyllis knew I would say no if she had asked, so she elected to do it anyway when I wasn't there. They're a nightmare because the dang cellar spiders love them.

Almost as if she were embarrassed by her admission of not wanting me to move out she clears her throat and puts on a haughty manner, "That's all one had to declare. See you on the 'morrow."

I sigh.

I'm about to turn back to my smutty book when I hear a rapid knock on the front door. Walking over I reluctantly open the door, I have a bad feeling, a low buzz in my chest, but I am curious. When I open the door stood in front is a statuesque brunette woman wearing a trench coat; her lips are painted in striking red lipstick. Femme fatale red. She has a slightly crazed look in her eye. What's more, I recognize her. It's the lady who was staring at us from across the road after Jai and I went skating.

CHAPTER 14

Jai

I go home to pack my stuff so that I can make my way to Zasha's. Brimming with anticipation I can't wait to see her, smell her hair as I press her body into mine. I would kiss her, learn her every intimate nook while I listen to her tell me all about her day, then curl into me at night.

Getting home something feels unhinged and a thrum of dread crawls up my spine, like a slasher horror. There's no Nellie, the lights are off and her door is open. But so is mine. My heart hammers, have we been robbed or worse? I hurry to my room and there are papers scattered everywhere, as if someone was searching for something. The chair to my desk is upside down and my gaming rig -which I've been upgrading piece by piece over the past year- has been pushed over. I flinch at that. That has surely just been done out of spite, or rage, maybe both.

On my desk there is a knife stuck through a bit of paper. Looking at it, it's the printed Rent-A-Romance profile of Zasha with her address and details. My heart hammers. Something about that knife in my room turns my stomach.

Fuck. Nellie did this. I knew I should have moved out the moment that we broke up.

Panicking I call Zasha. If Nellie did this I don't know what else she's capable of. The phone rings out.

I text Zasha. The ticks on the messaging app indicate that my messages have been read, but there is no response yet from Zasha.

Rushing out the door and getting on my bike I peddle with fury to Zasha's house. It's the quickest way without a car. I nearly get into an accident dodging a red light.

Then I arrive in her front garden; her house is eerily silent. What's going on?

Zasha

~One hour earlier~

Her name is Nellie.

She's Jai's girlfriend, or was, until she found out he had been cheating…on her with me. So here she is. On my doorstep. Great.

"…yes we're still boyfriend and girlfriend, engaged actually. We were always twin flames. We even bought a home together a few months ago. I'm heartbroken, absolutely heartbroken that he has a mistress," Nellie is eerily calm for someone who has found out something so devastating. But I can't judge, maybe she's in shock.

Every part of me feels betrayed, my body, my mind, my heart. No part of my instinct saw this coming. I felt so *safe* with him. How did he make me feel so safe?

Nellie brings out her phone and taps a few buttons. She's on Faceshare; the most popular social media app. Goodness knows how many followers she's reaching out to.

She has the video recording on her phone and is fluttering her eyelashes. She straightens her arm -raising it above her head- and pouts into the phone. Still in shock I just stare on agog, feeling so small. The incredibly shrinking woman. The incredibly gullible woman.

Nellie throws me a disdainful look as she monologues into her phone, "So here I am, at my fiance's mistress's lair. It's so sad when women go out of their way to hurt other women just because they are desperate-"

"- I didn't know!" I plead.

"-and so, so lonely. It's pitiful really. They shacked up because my fiancé was working behind my back for Rent-A-Romance, doing goodness knows what to so many women. Isn't that gross? My fiancé the gigolo. Well, I guess that's just Jai Maddox for you. Let me spell it, J-A-I…M-A-D-D-O-X! He's on Face Share for anyone interested. Anyway signing off hashtag Rent-A-Romance, hashtag Jezehell, hashtag cheaters gonna cheat."

Shaking, I've never felt so humiliated. Not even when Aunt Bernice used my photo for her dating profile to catfish for sexy hookups. How could Jai do this to me? How could he expose me to this?

Nellie slips her phone into her pocket and sneers at me, "Hmm. I always thought that if Jai was ever ridiculous enough to cheat on me, *me*…it would be with someone pretty. He must have felt sorry for you. Oh well. He's not worth it."

Normally I would brush off such a bitchy remark, but I feel so exposed, so it stings right in my heart. There I am standing in my pyjamas, nightgown and with hot oil dripping down my face, feeling very foolish for liking the wrong man…for liking the man who has bruised me from the inside out.

Nellie looks me up and down, smirks and then sashays off. Phyllis was right. Jai isn't worth it. Then the emotions overwhelm me and I break down crying. Now thanks to Nellie's Faceshare, the whole world knows what a fool I have been.

Jai

~One hour later~

I go up to the front door, and then I knock. No response. Peeking into the windows for the front room of the house I see a movement behind the curtains. My heart leaps. But why isn't anyone answering?

Calling Zasha's phone I hear it ring out. So I call again, but this time it goes straight to voicemail. Weird. Has she turned the phone off, or…blocked me? Nah. Why would she do that?

Something feels off. Should I call the police? What if Nellie's hurt her? With this thought, I pry open the door's letterbox. Crouching down I shout through it, "Zasha, you there? Are you okay?"

I just want to make sure she is safe. That's all. All the better if I can wrap my arms around her, feel her nestle into me. But…she just needs to be okay.

No one responds, however, I hear the gentle pitter-patter of footsteps and then an exhausted sigh.

Fuck, what the hell? If someone is in there but ignoring me, that can't be good. I can't imagine Zasha or her housemate ignoring me, why would they?

Opening the flap wider I bellow, "Nellie, you better not have hurt her. I'm bashing down the door!"

I try opening the door using the handle, and when that doesn't work I start bashing my shoulder against the front door. It doesn't budge but I am making a lot of noise.

Then I hear a shrill cry, it's Phyllis, "Away with ye red villain! Daren't ye darken our doorstep!"

Why is she pissed at me? Her housemate is not scaring me off, "Not going anywhere without seeing Zasha."

"Neigh! Take flight whoreson, we scorn ye!" Phyllis hisses with particular passion.

"She's there then? What happened?" Curious as to what has gone down I try and look through the letterbox, but I can only see a slither of darkened hallway.

Phyllis says sarcastically, "Your *enchanting* fiancé –"

"Fiance? I don't have a fiancé, what do you mean?" a dread seeps into my chest. I think I know what's going on but first I want to hear it from Phyllis, or better yet, Zasha.

"Nellie. Aah, a telltale heart was she, beating fresh at our door!" it's not very easy conversing with Phyllis, I need Google Translate.

Everything clicks. The final knife strike. God. Serves me right from not getting myself the fuck away from Nellie the moment I broke things off.

"Nellie came round? She's not my fiancé, we just live together."

Then I hear a chuckle; low, sardonic, bitter. I feel relief though, it's Zasha, "You *just* live together? Do you think we're stupid? Admit it Jai, she's your fiancé!"

I am still shouting through the letterbox, "Please Zasha, open the door! I'll explain everything. Nellie and I… we're not going out anymore. Please, you have to believe me!"

Feeling desperate I get up, looking around the street to refocus my vision and run my fingers through my hair in desperation. How can I prove that I have nothing to do with Nellie, even though we live together?

I hear the door crack open, and see a slither of Zasha's lovely face through the door; her face is wet from tears. She keeps the door on the safety chain as if I were a danger to her. A pang of pity courses through me. I can't stand to see her like this.

She looks at me wearily, "Uh huh. Jai, you know she's put it all on Faceshare ?"

"Yeah, what she said?" I don't use Faceshare but I'm morbidly curious as to what Nellie's been up to online.

"That I knew about it, you being with her, so it makes me your mistress, that I'm desperate. Jai, why didn't you just tell me about her?" Her voice sounds so fragile. My emotions come crashing down into a dark whirlpool, how can I fix this? *Can* I fix this?

Wishing I could suck out the poison that I've tainted her with, in desperation I raise my voice to convey the truth, end this madness, "It's not true though Zasha! I would never cheat, never on anyone, especially never on you. No one else even matters when I am with you."

Zasha snorts softly and starts to close the door, "Sure, goodbye Jai."

I don't want her to close the door on me. So, somewhat stupidly I jam my hand through the crack of the door, "Don't close the door on me Zasha, please. Zasha, give me a chance!"

"Okay, you can come in," she says, appearing to open the door and fiddle with the chain.

Surprised that it was that easy but instantly relieved, I remove my hand in anticipation of being allowed in. That's when she slams the door shut.

"Fuck…" I turn around, my back pressed to the door as I look up at the low grey sky.

I should go home. Try again in the morning.

But I'm not going anywhere. Zasha isn't getting rid of me just like that.

Because I need her.

Because I'm mad about her.

CHAPTER 15

Zasha

Sometimes, there is that brief moment when you wake up when you're not sure who you are, or even where you are, as your consciousness shifts from the realm of slumber to that of the living. I am trying to cling onto that feeling; that just woke up feeling, that don't know where I am feeling. It's a Tuesday and I don't want to go to work, I barely want to move a limb. Heavy from sorrow, I just want to inhabit this bed and stare at the ceiling. Sometimes a flash, a memory of my encounter with Nellie impinges with painful lucidity and I feel so mortified, as if I could drown. Sometimes Jai's visage inevitability materialises in my mind's eye like an apparition; achingly striking, painfully deceptive.

I hear a knock at the door, Phyllis comes in, "Cup of tea milady?" she comes tottering in and sets a cup of Earl Grey tea on my bedside table.

"Thank you," I manage to croak out. Sitting up, I take a sip of tea and look at Phyllis who is gazing at me with pity.

She pats my head, "Bed rotting, not a good look. Get some clothes on and get to work. It will take your mind off," that must be the most I've ever heard her speak without ye olde speech. It's disconcerting. I must be in an exceptionally sad state.

"Unless my colleagues have seen Nellie's Faceshare. Fuck, it's going to ruin my life." I say.

Phyllis shrugs, "And so what if they do? They can't fire you because of that. Right?"

I flap a hand hopelessly in lieu of words. I have no clue what my company's policy is on these things. The truth is that the real sting is being used by Jai; my mind doesn't quite compute it, nor does my body. But a girl needs to look at the evidence, and the evidence against Jai isn't good. He never told me he was living with Nellie.

Something tells me as well that there is more that he is hiding.

In the end, I heed Phyllis and get changed. Phyllis works from home, but as usual, she is dressed to the nines in Edwardian gear. Slinging my large backpack on I pry open the front door.

I nearly trip over a homeless man strewn on our door mat outside, with an empty bottle of cider by his head.

Oh, wait. That's…

"Jai! What the hell?" I am so mad at him, but a little part of me is thrilled that he's sleeping inebriated on my doorstep, *for me*. Still, I quickly step over him and march on. He's broken my heart, cheated on me, made me open season for humiliation – he is everything I don't need. Just looking at him I feel a throb from within my chest, as if I am bruised from the inside. Artfully hopping over his prone state, I see his hand attempt to precariously clutch at my ankle. Walking briskly to the front gate I don't look back.

"Fuck, Zasha! No hold on!" he scurries up.

"So you got drunk on my doorstep? Classy, is that because your fiancé chucked you out?" I taunt as I walk down the road as fast as I can. He'll catch up with me, he has long legs.

"Nah, that was a bottle someone chucked at my head, thought I could use it as a pillow. I wanted to talk to you is all," Jai says hurriedly.

He catches up with me and captures my wrist. His fingers on my skin emit a tingle that courses right through to my core. I hate him for this body betrayal. How can I still want him after what he has done?

His eyes bore into mine with steely determination, "Nellie's a liar. I'm not seeing her, and I'm not her fiancé, or anything else. I live with her because I was stupid enough to get a joint mortgage with someone who wasn't right for me."

I mutter darkly at him, "Why not just stay with your Dad then? Doesn't he live in London?" wrestling my wrist from his grip, I scurry as fast as I can go. However it is no effort for him to keep up. He just gently strides. Damned tall people.

"My stepmother doesn't like me being at home," he says with an underlying fragility. His fingers brush my wrist again, but he doesn't try to hold onto me. He just wants me to listen.

Stopping I look him in the face, what do I say to that, about his stepmother? My heart splits slightly for Jai. He sounds like he is telling the truth.

But then before I soften too much something occurs to me, "Why did you pretend you didn't recognise Nellie when we saw her after the massage parlour? Why didn't you just tell me then?"

"I didn't want her to ruin the time we were having."

Hmm, cocking my head to one side I wonder whether to give him the benefit of the doubt. I want to believe him, a little part of me *does* believe him, but it just seems strange he lied about that, and he never told me he was living with Nellie. Also, she seemed to truly believe she was…entitled to Jai. Why else would she do something so horrible as that Faceshare broadcast on my doorstep?

"Stop following me Jai. I need to go to work," my voice has a warning growl to it, he steps back as if he understands that I mean it. I don't want him to follow me. Hurrying my pace I burst into tears once I sense that I have cleared enough distance. He doesn't get to see what he's done to me.

"Zasha! Zasha!" he calls after me, his voice echoing down the grey street.

He lets me go.

I am glad.

I am disappointed.

Thankfully at work no one seems aware of my name being dragged through the mud on Faceshare. I breathe a little easier for now. However the paranoia still seeps, and I am still pissed at Jai, at how he has manipulated the whole Rent-A-Romance situation. Yeah sure he paid me all that money back, but even that seems fishy. I decide to go and see Hamish after work. He shouldn't be running an operation where sex and romance are intertwined. It's just wrong. I wonder how many of his clients are ensnared in this nightmare.

Sitting at the Rent-A-Romance office I see a couple of women studiously avoiding eye contact. Just like the first time I was here. I regret the first time I came here, paying for my own headfuck.

A speaker crackles with Hamish's voice, "Come in molasses mama."

Given that the other women in this room are white, that special greeting must be for me.

I'd rather not be alone in the room with Hamish, but hey ho.

Going through the door, Hamish is stroking his oxygen tank thoughtfully, like it's a cat, or beard. He gasps for air, puts his oxygen mask on and inhales, puts that down and then seemingly out of nowhere, finds a cigarette and puts it in his mouth.

Curious as to why he literally plays with fire I have to know if he's aware what he is doing is foolish, "Why do you do that? Breathe in the pure oxygen and then the cigarette, aren't you worried about explosions, about dying?"

"Nah, I'm worried about not living long enough to finish this packet of smokes," Hamish pulls out a cigarette package and then shakes it as if there were precious gems contained.

Ah well, we all have our priorities. Sighing gently I sit in the chair opposite.

"So, what can I do you for today?" Hamish leans back, puffing his cigarette.

"So the Rent-A-Romance experience, between Jai and I? It's been...*intense*," I make a *yeesh* expression with my face, to convey something dramatic has been going down.

Hamish cocks an eyebrow, "Oh, how you mean?"

"Well, you know," leaning forward I wink slowly and with great exaggeration at Hamish. Jai said this couldn't be an explicit conversation, the sex stuff at Rent-A-Romance is on the down low.

Hamish looks at me blankly, so I wink even more slowly.

"You don't mean, *hanky panky*?" he says to me, but much to my surprise he's horrified.

"You had better not mean *hanky panky*!" Hamish gets up from his chair, his fists balled with indignity.

"And what if I do?"

"Well, lemme tell you, someone is gonna be in trouble. Rent-A-Romance is clean, no sex, just romance. Okay? Geez!" Hamish looks genuinely upset.

Wait, but, does this mean Jai lied about this too? What kind of man have I fallen for?

After that, I received profuse apologies from Hamish but I had to get away.

With my head spinning from all of Jai's lies I stumble out of Rent-A-Romance. That's when my face lands smack into a wall of unnaturally tanned muscle peeking through an unbuttoned white shirt. In December. Looking up I see Magnus grinning down, his very white teeth gleaming.

"Well *hello*," Magnus purrs, his paw hand cupping my shoulder. I feel nothing but numb confusion.

To keep those impending tears at bay, I try to compose myself as my lips go wobbly and I sniffle. Magnus doesn't seem to notice, "Hey beautiful, so I've been meaning to ask…would you like to go out on a date? I would understand if you say no, as I know you have some stuff going on with Jai."

"No I don't. I don't have stuff with Jai, not anymore," that's when I start crying. Bawling in fact; my nose runnier than the Olympics. I wipe my snotty nose with the back of my hand leaving a distinctive snail trail. So gross, not exactly an elegant vision of a damsel in distress.

"Oh no, what is going on here? Don't cry; shush, shush, shush… shush." Magnus wraps his arms around me before I can extract myself. It's like being trapped in a beef cage. I try and squiggle out but he doesn't seem to notice.

"Perfect, just perfect," Magnus purrs with a faraway look in his eyes. Who is he talking to? Me? I look up; he is looking straight over my shoulder. Turning to look at who he is complimenting, I see he is gazing at his own reflection in the double-glazing of the front door entrance. Magnus's ideal partner is…Magnus.

That's when I hear Jai bellow aggressively, "Oi! What's this?"

Panicked, I try to work my way of out Magnus's grasp, I don't know why. Jai has forfeited his right to give a hoot what I am up to. Magnus doesn't let up however, instead, he squeezes me tighter.

"It's whatever I want it to be Jai," I say, still trying to break free of

Magnus.

Jai faces up to Magnus, his brows knitted together, "Let go of her, she doesn't want you to touch her. Alright?" Jai gets face-to-face, toe-to-toe with Magnus, which means I am stuck in between an angry man sandwich. I duck out of Magnus's arms and get out from the side, escaping the claustrophobic situation.

"Face it mate, she's not interested," Jai squares up. A terrible thought occurs given that violence could erupt, but this tussling over me is kind of hot.

"There is no way she can be interested in you and not *me*," Magnus is not lacking in self-regard.

"Don't work that way. Zasha's mine, and even if she wasn't, learn to read a woman. Alright?" Jai retorts possessively.

Claiming me in such feudal fashion as his own is a little tone-deaf after the proceedings of the last couple of days, but this doesn't stop my breath from hitching and my feelings soaring. Stupid me.

Magnus chuckles. He then wags his finger at Jai as if he is about to say something before walking away, "Ah Jai, sure, you have this one but rest assured that a man like you never wins," he then laughs manically to himself and swaggers off. That man has some serious baddie vibes.

Jai turns around and looks at me, "Zasha. You know I'm not giving up on you, right? I have this meeting and then I'm coming back to your front doorstep."

Jai's eyes softly meet my gaze. Leaning towards me he tries to grab my hand but I snatch it away, our fingers momentarily brushing against one another, "You lied to me Jai! You're not supposed to sleep with me at all! What, you thought you'd give yourself job perks?"

Jai frowns, "Hey, that's not exactly how it happened is it? If I recall a certain little lady pounced on me and then asked me what my prices were! You forced me into giving you my body!"

I laugh incredulously, placing each hand on my hips, "Oh ho ho! Now there is some revisionist history! Whatever next? You're going to tell me that Waterloo station was so christened by Abba?"

"Only if you tell me that Paddington station was named after a Peruvian bear," Jai looks at me intensely before he smiles, making my spirit rise like the sun on a cold day.

Trying to suppress his effect on me I say as calmly as I can muster, "You're kidding right?"

"Course I am," he smiles even more cheekily. My heart hammers. Dear God, I *do* want to pounce him.

"You're the one who ripped my bodice open, what was that for, a sneak peek?"

"It was to save your life actually as you were collapsing all over the place. Anyway, I remember you told me to pillage you," Jai's breathing is growing ragged, as is my own. On this cold winter day our breath turns the air in front of us to huffs of cloud, infusing into one another. He draws closer. Just remembering what we have been up to this past month makes me feel more than a little peckish for him.

Then I hear Hamish call out the front door, "Jai! Jai! Get in here you son of a bitch!"

Jai pulls an expression but before he heads over to an angry Hamish he turns to me, "I'm coming for you Zasha Williams, you're not getting away that easily."

Grimacing I feel torn apart by the conflict of emotions. No matter how much I fancy him, I am not ending up with a cheater. That's not my type of scoundrel.

Jai

Even though she hates me, every time I see Zasha it still perks me up. I mean, she could be flinging tomatoes in my direction and it still wouldn't put me off her. It might even be a new fetish…and free food.

Hamish's grating voice snaps me out of my thoughts as I linger reluctantly by his office door, "Get in here you schmuck! Sit!" I sit in the chair opposite his desk.

He is rasping in air through his oxygen mask. I have never seen him so worked up, "You're a damned liar Jai! Bringing this fine business into disrepute."

He is shaking. He means this.

"You've been giving hanky panky all over town under the Rent-A-Romance brand. Turning it to *caca*," weirdly, even though Hamish is a sleaze and I'm not exactly gelling with the other Romancers I feel a weight of guilt. He's genuinely upset.

Even if Hamish fires me, which I will deserve, I just want to apologise, "Hamish I -"

"No! You listen to me, you're not coming to Lapdance in Lapland on Friday! You're not coming to anything! You're fired!" he leans forward and wags his finger, before collapsing back into his chair and grabbing the mask, gasping for air again. I'm not sad I no longer have to eat greasy finger food off an exploited woman. I am however sad that Hamish is in such bad shape over everything.

Feeling remorseful, I decide to wait it out to make sure he has captured his breath before I leave. My pockets are emptier – as I gave Zasha what she paid, which was more than I was paid. I don't have a home I want to go to, and Zasha is more pissed with me than I know what to do with. But even if she refuses to talk to me ever again, at least I got to meet someone amazing, got to connect with someone who made me lose my head.

And I'm still not giving up on her.

When Hamish regains his composure, I quietly get up and walk towards the exit.

Looking over my shoulder before I leave for good, I apologise, "Sorry I did that to you Hamish. But you know what? I met the most incredible woman of my whole life. So yeah, even if I've lost her, it was all worth it to know she was out there. So thanks for that."

Then I step out the door.

That evening -after packing my essentials from home while Nellie is still at work- I go to the office. I swear the Japanese knotweed problem has gotten exponentially worse over the last few days. Sunil and Chantelle have used the office machete to hack away the worst of it around their desk. Sunil told me they don't mind living around it because they raid the office beer fridge at night and get drunk.

It would be awkward to join them in this. Plus, the way they look at each other I am beginning to suspect I am an unwanted fellow office squatter. Don't know why, maybe because they're so used to having the whole place to themselves at night. Such workaholics.

I lay my sleeping bag on top of the knotweed under my desk and get in, fully clothed. The sharp fluorescent lights of the office automatically turn on when someone moves, so I put my arm over my eyes to shield them so I can attempt sleep.

Sunil whispers loudly to Chantelle, "He's asleep, we can now try that wheelbarrow position we saw the other day."

"Oh my! Sunil! Are you sure he's asleep?"

"Yeah. I'm sure."

Then lots of snogging sounds ensue, then wet sounds, then sex sounds. They are moving around the room a lot, which means they are probably sitting their bottoms on a fair few desks. Dave is a neat freak, this would upset him.

I suddenly really need to relieve myself but I don't want to move. It would be awkward for Sunil and Chantelle to know I know they're shagging. Moving my arm I crack open an eye expecting to catch sight of the errant love birds. Instead a dozen green bugs with big eyes and pincers stare back at me, looking extra big because they're right in my face.

Scrambling away I shout, "What the fuck!"

Chantelle and Sunil leap up in surprise. Chantelle does a rubbish job of trying to cover her tits with her hands in a panic, Sunil makes a lame attempt to shield his willy. They're as naked as a politician in a sex dungeon.

"It's not what it looks like, really it's not!" Sunil squeaks.

"Ohmygawd Jai! You're awake!" exclaims Chantelle.

Yeah, no shit. I only closed my eyes for all of three seconds before they decided to have a spin on each other.

"Yeah I am, and we have visitors," inspecting the tiny alien invaders it becomes apparent that they are praying mantises. How did they get here? It's not quite up there with the parakeets of London, but still.

Sunil relaxes, now just covering his dick with one hand, "Uh yes, we have an infestation of them. They came with the Japanese knotweed Graham planted. He says they must have hopped out of his pocket."

I groan. Nestling back into my sleeping bag I flap my hand over my eyes once more in an undoubtably rubbish attempt to get some sleep. I don't give a fuck anymore about being a zoo exhibit for tropical insects. We do it to them. It's fair.

I hope this is my rock bottom. I have a hunch it's not.

"He's asleep again! Hop on then!" I hear Sunil whisper loudly.

Just. Kill. Me.

When I awake I write a note for Zasha in the office and then stroll down to a nearby French delicatessen to buy a box of macarons. I don't know why people go mad over macarons -

they're overpriced sweetie sandwiches. I hope though that they show Zasha how much I want her.

Making my way to Zasha's I think about what I plan to do every day until she forgives me. I'll deposit gifts and notes until she at least gets so fed up that she talks to me, if only to tell me to bugger off.

At her house I knock on the door, but no one answers.

So I bellow, "Zasha! I know you're in there. Still not giving up on you. Read my note!"

Silence. I sigh loudly in exacerbation and then carefully post the macarons and note through the door.

Hoping she will come sauntering through the door I sit outside.

I'll do this every day before the start of my work day.

"I'm not giving up on you Zasha Williams! Do you hear?" Shouting, I rest my head against the door as I wait, I still have time until work.

After ten minutes or so a police car screeches by and two burly officers come out, "Sir, are you the one bothering this household?"

My heart skips a beat, rock bottom would definitely be getting a criminal record out of this, "Yeah I am."

"Well this is your last warning, we're going to have to ask you to move. Step away from this house sir and don't bother them again, do you understand?"

I nod, but now I feel despair. Does Zasha feel so stalked that she called the police? Fuck.

I get up with the stern police officers watching me. Zasha's next-door neighbour -an old lady with a cup of tea and rollers in her hair- comes out and scowls royally in my direction. Not the walk of shame I'd hoped for.

Fuck 'em all.

Still not giving up on Zasha.

CHAPTER 16

Zasha

After I saw Jai at the Rent-A-Romance office I just couldn't take it anymore. All torn up, I needed to get out of my house, get out of London, get out of the country, and hide for a while. Barbados brings me back to life, so I booked a last-minute flight to visit. My work were not exactly understanding, but I explained I would work remotely. Although they were hardly happy with that either. Oh well, sometimes a girl just needs to look after herself.

But I am not going to see my parents, absolutely not. I love my mum but she triumphs in my failures. No, instead I will spend the time with my lovely but predatory Auntie Bernice. Her house size is a small fraction of the palatial size of my parent's estate and is on the other side of the island, but I feel so much more at home at Auntie's.

When Auntie Bernice talks about relationships with me she goes full Patois, "When you gwaan find yo'self a bossman huh? Com'mon chile! Yuh gwaan die ah virgin!" At first, the questions about when I was going to start dating were relentless. I suspect because she wanted to hit the clubs with me.

So yup, initially she was a little intense. But then when I explained that I had been briefly seeing someone I thought liked me but was actually a love cheat, she completely got it and was so kind. We took walks on the beach and drank cocktails made by her favourite barmen. Many of whom she goosed while slipping tips into their trunks; in the process of groping for another type of tip altogether.

She gave me lots of tea, stuffed me with plantain and pepper pot stew and restored me.

So after a couple of weeks I went back home.

When I arrive back home in the UK, Phyllis greets me warmly, presenting me with a creepy-looking sack doll with button eyes that she has made, "It's for you. A most cherished little friend. It shall keep you company until the end of your days, as will I," taking the doll I try not to stare at it for too long, in case it comes to life and decides to hunt me down and wear my skin.

"Thanks Phyllis, what a special gift. Anything else happen?" a part of me hopes so much that Jai has been reaching out, trying to say sorry for being a scumbag.

"No, nope, nothing. Nothing at all," her eyes dart evasively. She then walks backwards into her bedroom and closes the door. Shady. Hmm.

I've blocked Jai's number. But now I unblock it.

He can't have forgotten about me already…could he?

A week goes by and I hear and see nothing of Jai. Disappointment sinks in…he's lost interest. He has upended my life, brought turmoil and heartbreak and has now just lost interest, as if I were just a thing to be discarded. I don't even know where he lives. I guess I could call him, but that's not right, that boy should be grovelling to me.

Going to work every morning I feel numb, it is hard to believe that he has given up this quickly. But I guess it's just his true colours showing. It doesn't make it easier. It stings more, to be honest.

But then, he gave me all that money back. If I didn't matter, he wouldn't have done that, right? *Right*? Unless he was just getting his kicks.

Checking my phone nearly every minute I am disappointed that he hasn't messaged since I unblocked him.

Maybe it's natural that he just gave up. I was just a lark to him. Someone to fill the time before he married his fiancé Nellie.

I am so confused.

I thought there was something real between us.

Jai

At work all I can think about is Zasha. The good times, the current shit times. It's wrecking me. Sat at my knotweed-captured desk with my sleeping bag tucked next to my feet I have my headphones on as I work on the cinematics for the latest game in development. It's supposed to be a light-hearted adventure game for children; but I've saturated the screen with blood red and added some sad clowns as background NPCs, like my inner turmoil. Praying mantises scuttle over my desk, sometimes congregating to peer at my grim countenance.

Every day for two weeks during my lunch break I have been posting little presents that fit through Zasha's letterbox; usually chocolates, or macarons. She hasn't called the police on that yet at least.

Zasha hasn't messaged me either so, you know, who knows? I'm just going to keep going like the lovesick loser that I am.

Her phone is blocked so that's a non-starter. I was messaging her like crazy until I realised it was like screaming into a void.

A hand claps my shoulder and Dave's voice booms from behind, "Now this, this is the work of a man who has had his heart shredded. Nice doom and gloom there Jai. What next? Some flying skulls and pentagrams? Geez this game is for five-year-old girls, not grown men who've fucked up."

I groan and slouch into my chair, "*Fuckkk*, I'm losing it."

Dave pats his hand paternally on my shoulders, "Hey, it's okay, it's okay. In fact Jai Maddox my man, have I got a treat for you. You have had a tough time over the past two weeks. *Sooo*....we've got you a nice spa experience. They're coming to pick you up soon. What do you say?"

This makes me perk up. It's also nice to feel appreciated.

"Yeah, sure," shrugging as non-committedly as I can, I actually kind of want to sob into Dave's Christmas jumper and tell him that he is God. However I don't see a route for how doing that will get me Employee of the Month.

Dave perks up but there is a glint in his eye that I cannot quite read, "Okay, great! I'll call back and confirm."

So there I am standing like a twerp outside the office, hands stuffed in the pockets of my jeans. Oooh a spa! Never been to one of those before. Yeah, there are my sports massages at Tantric Touch, but they don't count.

Dave told me the car was coming to get me any minute now.

A car slows down. It's a black car with tinted-out windows. Weird.

Not an Uber, not a taxi. Well, anyway, I get to skive off work with the boss's permission!

Approaching the car, I watch as it slows and the doors open.

"Hey up!" I greet cheerily. However, three muscular men in black cat burglar outfits emerge. Magnus, Roman and Kwame. They are all grinning. Fucking menacing.

Nah! Nah way mate.

"Hello Jai, Papa sent us to look after you. You see, we tie up loose ends here at Rent-A-Romance, and you're looking rather loose to us," they chuckle like sinister hyenas. Fuck this. I'm out of here!

Scarpering to run, one of the Romancers tackles me, leaping on my back, right there on the busy streets of London. People here don't bother helping if you're being mugged unless you look like a millionaire who might richly reward them. Given the friendliness of Londoners, it's a small blessing that no one comes to join in the violence.

As I lie on the floor I feel a cloth pressed to my mouth and then I black out.

Waking up later crouched in pitch blackness, I try to move my hands but I cannot, and I can't seem to get enough air. There is something on my head.

"Oi, anyone out there?" I shout.

Silence.

"Come on, let me go! I won't tell a soul what's happened."

Nothing. But then I hear footsteps and mumbling.

Excited I try and thump against the container I am in. God, I can barely breathe.

That's when my ears tune into the sound.

TICK, TICK, TICK

It's coming from my wrists...is that....a bomb?

I hear a voice - Magnus, "He's awake. Did you say we could release it in the form of gas using the remote?"

"Yeah, just press the red button. Always press the red button. Makes life more interesting," says Hamish.

Then my world goes dark.

CHAPTER 17

Zasha

It's impossible to ignore the fact that Phyllis is acting rather evasively. Every once in a while I see her stalking about nervously in our living room, munching delicately on a macaron while twirling whatever parasol matches her outfit for the day. When she sees me she squeaks and retreats to her bedroom. Hm.

I've been putting up Christmas decorations, to take my mind off Jai. The radio silence from him hasn't stopped bothering me. I think about him all the time and hope that he is okay.

Even though he hurt me.

Even though he doesn't care.

Phyllis would usually help with the Christmas tree, but given that she's decided she has an allergy to my presence that's not happening. I think about calling my Awkward Squad girls but I am still too embarrassed to tell them about what has happened with Jai. Soon. I'll tell them soon. Instead, I have to make do with the company of my sack doll. I made a little Christmas hat for it and have taken to carrying it around in my pocket for company. Yup. I'm now officially a side-kick human goon to a possibly haunted doll.

Usually I love this time of the year. The smells of Christmas... cloves, clementines, cinnamon, pine. Talking of pine, usually every year we acquire a Christmas tree for the living room. This year however I had to lug it for a mile down the road by myself. I felt every painful step, with the pines pressing into my shoulder and neck like a depressing Last Temptation of Christ replay. All the while, all I could think about was Jai. I liked him, and still do. It hurts, to have been used that way, manipulated and lied to. And the way he lies, it's so believable.

Sighing, I pause on my current task of hanging baubles on the Christmas tree and try to gather my thoughts. Wearing a Christmas jumper and a gold paper crown as I listen to holiday tunes, I still can't get my heart to play ball with me. No amount of glitter, twinkle, fluff or tinsel can obscure the painful reality that I am in tatters, like an exploded balloon.

A tear creeps down my face, I wipe it.

That's when I hear the knock.

Opening the door much to my surprise I see Hamish dressed as Santa, his little gas tank under one arm, cigarettes in another. He is reinforced by burly Romancers dressed as Santa's little helpers in stripy tights and little hats with bells, including Magnus who is pouting and holding a tablet. In front of them all is a suspiciously ginormous gold parcel topped with the biggest green shiny bow. Passersby from the street are gathering to gawk. Great, just what I need. An audience. Lovely.

Hamish is grinning with particular menace, what have we here?

"Ho ho ho! Merry Christmas sunshine…boy oh boy have we got a swollen package for you!" Hamish enthuses before dragging on a cigarette and spluttering into my face.

"Nope," I say and start closing the door as briskly as I can.

Magnus steps forward and forces the door open.

"You're going to want to hear us out," Magnus demands with great severity to his tone.

Just what I need, ultimate mansplaining on my doorstep.

"You have two minutes and then I call the police."

Hamish takes another drag of his cigarette and exhales, "Okay, well firstly. You're gonna wanna see this. Come here son," Hamish beckons Magnus, who rolls his eyes and presenting the tablet, navigates to Nellie's Faceshare page.

Hamish clears his throat, "Firstly, like, only three people follow naughty girl Nellie on Faceshare; her mama, papa and a guy called 'ToeLover81' – we know you've been worrying about that."

Okay, it hurt too much to check out Nellie's socials so that's a relief, at least this shameful event isn't there for all to behold. However, I still feel sad about being cheated on.

"But that's not the big deal. Press play Magnus," Magnus does the most exaggerated sigh and navigating to a video on Nellie's profile he presses play, shaking his head.

Nellie's shrill voice rings out in the video, "Wassup bitches and snitches. So some of you losers have been all 'Oh but didn't you break up with Jai already? How could he have cheated on you if he already dumped you?' Well fuck you! Guys don't get to break up with girls like me, that's not a thing! And, and… who would break up with all this hotness? Ooh ya!" Nellie in the video does a twirl and then a slut drop. Before blowing a big fat kiss to the screen.

"Wooo! Jai, how you going to be missing all of this? Huh? *Huh?* You must be cray-cray!" Nellie screeches.

My heart gladdens. Jai didn't cheat on me, or Nellie…or whoever. He was telling the truth. I feel a bit ashamed I didn't listen to him. But how was I to know? A girl has to look out for herself.

I smile and tilt my head.

Hamish licks his lips as my expression brightens, "Bet you're wondering what's in the box huh? Well, guess what suga' lumps, there is only one ending we have at Rent-A-Romance. Press the red button Kwame!"

Kwame smiling, presses the red button. Suddenly there is an

explosion of glitter and smoke from the box, and shouting, one man shouting.

"OHMYFUCKINGGAWDAREYOUINSANE?" out pops Jai, dressed like the mad king of Santa's helpers. He is bedecked in a festive elf's outfit and jingle bell hat, and covered head to toe in copious glitter. The crowd outside our house holler and whoops at this reveal.

"I'm blinded! I'm fucking blinded! The glitter's lacerating my eyes!" he cries out in breathless agony, his hands trying to rub the glitter off his face, but rubbing it in instead.

"Jai!" I cry out at this tortured, shimmery man.

"Zasha, you there?" he grasps blindly in front of me. I give him my hand and squeeze it reassuringly. He squeezes back and grins.

With his eyes still gummed over with glitter he asks, "Zasha… what's going on? Where am I? Hamish and his handsome pricks did this. They had me in handcuffs that dropped off when the glitter exploded in my face."

"Yeah, I know, they're stood around you. They also told me all about Nellie's lies," Magnus is shaking his head sassily and Hamish is grinning away. Hamish is loving this.

Jai perks up, "Oh brilliant! Well, losing one of my five senses is okay, if it means you'll stop ignoring me."

"Yeah, I unblocked my phone a while ago, but didn't hear from you," recalling the radio silence from Jai a resurgence of disappointment settles in my chest.

"Well, after you called the police on me –"

"Wait, I did what? I didn't do that!" I hear scurrying footsteps behind me. Hm, Phyllis.

"…and ignored my notes and all those gifts I sent."

"I didn't get any gifts, or notes for that matter, what do you mean?" this is all very confusing.

More scurrying in the background. I crane my shoulder back.

"Hey Phyllis, get over here," I shout. I have a hunch about what's going on.

"Greetings m'ilady…and Jai," his name rolls off her tongue with contempt.

"Phyllis. Did some things come through the door for me recently?"

"Perhaps. One cannot be certain," Phyllis swishes her hips.

"And what did you do with them?" I think back to Phyllis eating the macaron, she only ever eats scones and teacakes.

"Did you *eat them* Phyllis?"

"Oh Zasha dearest!" Phyllis runs over, panting away -likely because of her overly tight corset- and then throws herself dramatically against me with the back of her palm to her forehead. "I simply didn't want you to elope with this reprobate!"

"Phyllis. You are officially a rubbish housemate. Ugh," I shake my head.

"*Prithee* Zasha, *prithee*. I did it for your own protection, lest ye be enchanted," Phyllis pulls out a lace handkerchief and dabs it under her eyes, sniffling, even though there are no real tears.

Then she looks genuinely sad, "And I don't want to lose you as a housemate."

I say nothing, with her interference she *has* lost me as a housemate, but perhaps there is hope to salvage our friendship, despite that she ate all the macarons.

Hamish interjects looking at his Rolex watch, "Hey *señorita*, why don't you take this boy in, give him a wash and some of the old forced proximity if you know what I mean eh, eh?"

It seems unhealthy to take my romantic cues from Hamish, but I suppose that's what we've been doing all along.

Clearing my throat, I try to convey my genuine gratitude, "I appreciate you bringing Jai to me, although he might need to see a therapist or three at some point after today. Thank you Hamish, thank you lads."

Offering Jai my hand again he finally clambers out of the box. His long legs swinging out – bedecked with stripey tights. He is blinking rapidly, his eyes deep red and utterly covered in glitter. I really should take him to the hospital to get his eyes checked, or maybe call Nat, but I'll hose him down first. A wave of desire rolls through me at the thought.

"Thanks all," I wave, probably a bit too dramatically. The audience in front of my home has grown so large that it has now brought out the theatrics in me.

The crowd cheers and snap a bunch of pictures. Very embarrassing.

But at least I got my man.

Jai

After Zasha takes me in, she makes me climb into a bin bag and take my glittery clothes off. Phyllis didn't want me traipsing the glitter through the carpet.

At first, I was just in a state of fucking shock. I had the girl! Though I had been imprisoned against my will, drugged for several hours and forcibly stripped while unconscious and dressed as a festive elf... I had the girl!

Zasha runs the showerhead over my body. It's so good to feel the glitter washing off my face.

"Does that feel good?" Zasha asks as she basks me in warm water, angling it in particular at my abdomen. She is definitely perving on me.

"Yeah, but do you know what would feel even better?" I retort, my mouth tilting into a mischievous grin. I pry the shower head from her grip and place it back on it's holder. Zasha looks confused and then squeals in surprise when I capture her waist and drag her into the shower, kissing her with bruising intensity, covering her in all my glitter muck as I remove her clothes. She gasps as I strip her down, impatient to have her out of her clothes. I want to devour her like a hungry man. I need to feel our skin pressed against each other so closely that we meld.

Her nipples bud like pebbles the moment I have her out of her clothes. Then slowly, sensuously under the water, I kiss each stiff peak tenderly before gently biting a bud and stretching it with my teeth while watching her reaction, listening to her whimper incomprehensible nothings.

"I've missed this Zasha, missed you," I moan as I torment her.

She is as wet as I am hard when I grab her delicious, full bottom and spread her legs apart. Lifting her, I pin her against the wall.

"Yes Jai, yes," Zasha's voice is low and needy as she wraps her arms around my neck and buries her nose into the dip of my shoulder.

"Fuck, I need to get a condom" I breathe in, trying to regain my senses.

"Don't worry, I'm on birth control and I've been checked recently," Zasha moans.

"Okay, I was checked too," I manage to grunt.

Slowly I mount her onto my shaft; savouring her enveloping me, drinking me in with her tight, pulsating pussy. She arches her back as I burrow in so deep I can feel my cockhead gently rubbing against her cervix. I press her against the shower, kissing the fuck out of her, my tongue rudely snaking into her mouth, caressing her tongue. Then I pick up the pace and we fuck relentlessly as I plough her. We fuck so hard in the humid onslaught of the shower that our mutual moans and grunts become indistinguishable, an animalistic frenzy as we feast upon each other's drenched bodies. Feeling her tight walls fluttering around my cock once more is incredible. The last few weeks without Zasha have left me famished for her.

Every once in a while Phyllis politely knocks, "*Prithee*, no expression of fluids within the bathing quarters," we ignore her.

I capture Zasha's soft lips in a kiss as she gasps under my onslaught, so wet, pushing against me for more, "Oh my God Zasha, this is perfect, this is where you belong, around me. Drinking all of me in."

She then whispers wickedly into my ear while digging her nails into my back, "Or perhaps Jai you belong here, buried deep inside, fucking me like this for all of infinity."

God, I'm obsessed with her, so I grunt and gently biting her shoulder I feel a pressure build up in the base of my spine before my balls contract and I spurt hot jets of cum into Zasha. She rides me hard, panting as she does so, she looks as if she is dazed. Afterwards, as I soften, I place her back on her feet, but Zasha will never fuck me and walk away unsatisfied.

I turn her around, her delicious tits pressed against the wall.

Using my foot to tap her feet apart I whisper, "Did you think I would let you walk away without making you cum? Think again,"

Zasha gasps at my filthy words, "God Jai, you're a bloody rascal."

Craning my arm around her front, my finger finds her pussy and spreads her puffy swollen lips; rouged from being fucked. I dip three of my fingers into her pussy and use her sloppy wetness by rubbing her cream on my fingers and massaging her stiff clit. She moans and cranes her head back. With my other hand, I playfully pull Zasha's hair, making her gasp. As she does so, I plant greedy kisses along her arched neck while I rub her clit roughly in circular motions until she is pushing her plump bottom against my stirring cock. Dipping my fingers back into her soaked cunt, I rub the sensitive spot within. Soon Zasha starts to cry out incomprehensibly, riding my fingers as if they were my cock.

"That's it, fuck my fingers Zasha, make yourself cum,"

Zasha's body stiffens and then shudders as she cums hard around my fingers, squeezing her walls around them, milking them. She bites her lower lip from the intensity and her posture stiffens before she goes slack.

After that, we kiss in the shower. I cup both sides of her beautiful face with my hands and pull her towards me, planting kisses along her cheeks before capturing her mouth again.

I missed her so much, I never want to feel like that again.

A few days pass and I go into our local corner shop and spot a familiar face on the front of the Daily Mercury. It's a tabloid newspaper usually known for alerting the population to possible alien invasion, and the sexual peccadilloes of premier-league footballers. However, I am surprised to see the star of the newspaper. It's probably best not to tell Zasha that the Daily Mercury has her splashed on the front page, her breasts seemingly photoshopped to appear gargantuan with the headline, "*Extra Extra! Buxom Nerd Savaged by Elf off his Shelf!*" There is a smaller picture that shows me climbing out of the box, and with the clever photography, apparently grasping for Zasha and assaulting her chest-first. I'm just glad that it's hard to identify me as my face is covered in so much glitter that I resemble a festive disco ball. Poor Zasha though, can't say the same thing.

CHAPTER 18

Zasha

~One week before Christmas~

So Jai and I decided to rent together. It's been unkind to our pockets given that he's tied into a joint mortgage and I am effectively paying to rent two places until Phyllis finds a new housemate, but we're just about there. We found somewhere to live at short notice. It's not a nice place; creatures that resemble earthworms with legs emerge at night in the kitchen to snack on errant crumbs but hey – at least they're minding their business unlike our last housemates, and they don't eat all the macarons.

Anyway, there was no way I was forgoing an awesome Christmas tree; given that Phyllis undeservedly has the first one that I bought. So Jai and I have been decorating a brand new one that we've acquired. We've used decorations that represent our journey together; ice hockey skates, pirate flags, weird leather baubles for the dark romance and a few others. To be honest, we've turned it into a pretty odd-looking tree, but we love it.

It has been magical being with him for the past few weeks. My heart feels like it flips even harder the more I get to know Jai and grow comfortable being around him. It's hard to define just one thing that I like; it's the totality of him which pulls me in; his mischievous smile, the fire in his eyes, his dimples, his gloom and sweetness. I just sort of love him.

Sitting by the tree with my legs folded behind me after work,

I sup a very nice full glass of pinot noir. Gazing up, I admire the shimmering lights that we have wrapped around the tree. Wearing my Christmas hat, I feel particularly content. When we first met for the pirate romance scenario I felt like I was hot like a cozy hearth due to wearing too much synthetic fabric; today it is because I am basking in well love, even if he hasn't said the words yet. I at least feel that way about him.

The door opens in the hallway.

"Hey Jai, is that you?"

"Yeah, give me a minute. Just need to get changed."

Strange, usually he comes straight through and we kiss or christen a new bit of furniture.

Finally, after ten minutes he comes through, wearing the elf outfit he was presented in when he exploded out of the glitter box a few weeks ago. To be fair, he makes an extremely sexy elf, but then he makes a sexy everything.

I keenly sip my wine without losing eye contact before making my approval known, "Mm, mm, mm. What position will my big bad elf be in today?"

Grinning, Jai has come bearing a few gifts to be placed under the tree. He plonks most of them down next to me.

Dropping down to his knees on the floor, he sits beside me.

"So yeah, Zasha, you know I love ya," my heart leaps in elation at his words, even if they have been uttered with casual aplomb.

"No I didn't know that, because you've never said it."

"What? Sure I have, thought it loads," his eyes bore into mine, making my heart giddy-up. Living with him has only increased our passion for each other. We're having a grand old time, let's just put it that way.

"Well, I'm not telepathic Jai. It would be nice if you had used words to tell me, like I tell you all the time," I complain, imbibing more of my fine wine.

"Oi Zasha! What do you mean? You've never said you love me." His whole body unfurls in delight.

"Yes Jai, I have. I am very sure of it. I mean, why wouldn't I? I have been thinking it." Of course I told him, I must have. Right?

Jai shakes his head, his eyes glowing, "This is the first time you've ever told me. Just thought you wanted me for my body, and games console."

We look at each other and crack up laughing, falling backwards. With Jai on his back and looking so hot as an elf I decide to have my way with him. With a deft motion, I straddle him before arching down to capture his lips into a kiss.

"God I fancy you. Don't think we've christened the floor yet," I rub myself against his groin. Jai moans and grinds back. He puts his hands firmly on my thighs to still me, his fingers digging in. Frustrated I try to rock again but he stills me.

Groaning he says, "Uh, yeah so I uh. What was I going to do? Oh yeah."

His hand gropes the floor around, eventually his fingers hook around a small present. Much to my disappointment he lifts me gently off his torso and places me back on the floor. What an anti-climax.

But just as my heart is sinking from the brutal rejection Jai gets onto one knee, as if he were about to be knighted. I try and recompose myself as a beat hammers in my chest.

Clearing his throat he knits his brows together, "So uh, shit didn't think of the logistics of this. Uh, can you pull the bow, and uh, unwrap the pressie and hand it back to me please?"

"Yeah, yeah of course," I abide by this peculiar ritual and undoing the bow, gently pry apart the paper and then hand the box over back to Jai. My heart is galloping. Is he about to…? Surely not?

Jai clears his throat, "Zasha Williams…"

My eyes widen. They're about to fall out of my head. This isn't happening, I mean, we've only known each other for like five minutes!

He flips open the box and inside are twinkly, shiny...

Nipple clamps. Festive nipple clamps with bells.

I grimace at Jai, "You asshole!" I lightly hit his arm with the back of my hand.

Jai looks confused and then places the box aside hurriedly, "Uh… uh…wrong box!"

He scrambles and picks up another - the same size, same paper, same bow as the nipple clamp box.

He smiles extra cheekily at me; his eyes sparkling with merry mischief.

This time he unwraps the bow and paper himself and presents the box, "Yeah, uh Zasha Williams. I'm mad about you, sort of obsessed, to tell the truth. So uh-"

He flips open the box and there is a big ol' white gold ring with a chunky garnet stone at the centre.

My heart accelerates and I gasp.

"- can you marry me? You're so hot, and lovely, and it would kill me to ever lose you again," Jai's words are simple but they strike a deep chord that resonates, because it's exactly how I feel about him.

"Yeah, I'll marry you," I say trying to retain composure but feel thrilled inside. This is probably the worst idea…the guy is going to go running when he finally meets my family and sees the horror that it is to join the Williams family, but you know what? I am mad about Jai, my mum will just have to deal with it.

Jai throws himself at me and hugs me tightly.

"Hold out your finger then!" I hold out my hand as he plucks the ring out of the box and attempts to squish it onto my finger. It seems a bit small, my face turns red. What if it doesn't go on?

Jai pulls a face, "I've got something for that."

He runs out and returns with a tube of KY Jelly.

"Seriously?" This is going to be burnished as a forever memory. The time we got engaged and he had to force the ring on with sex lube.

He squishes the cold gel onto my finger, slathers it and then slips the ring on. He tries to wipe the lubricant off, but I shake my newly bejewelled finger at him.

"I have a better idea my baddie elf," Gently I push him back down onto the floor and nudge down his elf tights with his boxers.

Jai seems to be already sporting an erection – he looks at me sheepishly, "I got hard when you said yes."

I then whip off my clothes as if I'm now allergic to them.

Leaning over I kiss him as I wrap my hand around his erection, gently caressing his length, spreading that excess KY jelly over its length. Feeling his delicious girth I squeeze and slowly pump him. He moans underneath me, rutting the fist of my hand as we kiss, our tongues slipping against one another. His eyes flutter to a close, as if he were enraptured.

"Open your eyes Jai and look at me," I request.

As he does so his eyes lock onto mine.

"Fuck," he says as we moan and gasp and the lube on my hand meets the precum on the crown of his cock.

Breaking the kiss I whisper into his ear, "I love you… you do realise you're the best gift ever, don't you?"

Jai sits up, propping himself up by the elbows, "No, the honour the honour goes to you babe, each and every time."

I straddle his spread legs, feeling his dripping cockhead levelling with my core, before I take in his length, relishing the delicious discomfort as it spreads me apart. Placing my hands on his shoulders I kiss him feverishly while moving up and down with intentionally agonising slowness, grinding his cock against that sensitive spot within as my clit rubs against the thatch of hair covering his cock. Whimpering my eyes pin against his, his pupils drinking me in as we find our rhythm together, one rhythm. We move in tandem like this for a while, our bodies fused.

"Oh my gosh Jai, this is so good. God, I just want more," moaning I bounce vigorously on his swollen cock, my body pent up and begging for release as his warm lips seek out the crook of my neck.

"Well you would my greedy girl, wouldn't you? You will always want more," Jai groans wrapping his arm around my waist while his other hand caresses my breast, squeezing it roughly before flicking my stiff, plump nipple lazily with his thumb.

Jai moans as I slam up and down on his cock, my hands gripping his shoulders for leverage. His hand snakes down my belly to my soaked core before his thumb greets my clit, rubbing it roughly, tweaking the sensitive pearl of nerves. With this attention from him I am undone, and my body tips over the edge, awash with crashing cascades of sheer bliss. Soon I am coming all around him, squeezing like a vice. Milking him as my nails dig into his skin, burnishing imprints of half-moons on his broad shoulders.

"Oh God yes, Zasha, yes!" he groans, his fingers still taunting my nub, not letting up. His other hand is at my waist, gripping me this way he pumps me up and down on his cock, stoking his swollen shaft like he's trying to start a fire. Which is how I feel, like I'm on fire.

And then he bites my neck as he comes, making me clamp down even harder and buck against him, feeling his cock thicken within my tightness as I squeeze all around him. We move against each other, milking one another, satisfied, quivering wrecks. It feels wet underneath, then I realise Jai's thighs are covered in my cream.

He sees me gazing at what I have done. Finally, he traces his hand from my nub to the wetness on his leg. Dipping two fingers into my nectar he brings his fingers to his lips and licks them, as if tasting a delicacy. Inhaling a sharp intake of air, perfumed with our musky scent, I count my blessings I will have much more of this to come with Jai.

"Merry Christmas darling Zasha," Jai says as I shudder in his lap and wrap my arms around him.

You can't buy this kind of love. Well, you can, but it will set you back five thousand pounds.

EPILOGUE

Jai

It's been a blast since Zasha and I got engaged. We went to the Hyde Park Winter Wonderland, going on all the rides like maniacs, ice skating like loons and running around the town in reindeer ears. Then coming home and well, let's say everywhere has now been christened many times over. I could be nude together with her forever, if she'd let me…and if universal basic income was a thing. Although I'm still mulling suing Dave for conspiring with Hamish to falsely imprison me, so maybe dreams can come true.

I cannot wait for us to get hitched, I would do it tomorrow, but she wants to do it properly and have family, friends and all that. Not sure how I feel about that, because it's other people that make me nervous, they're the only thing that have ever fucked up Zasha and I. She hasn't met my Dad; we haven't met each other's friends, we've just been existing in our own cosy bubble since we moved in together. She will run a mile when she meets my family. She doesn't talk about hers, but if they're anything like her, they will be lovely and elegant.

I hear Zasha on the phone as I take her a hot chocolate and mince pie into our living room, "Yes mum, yes that is me on the front page. No mum my hair is not the most embarrassing part of that article. No, neither is my bum size thank you very much. No, I haven't spent all my early inheritance from Grandpa on new breasts, they used a computer to enlarge them. Who's the man assaulting me? Well, the funny thing is…he's my new fiancé! Did I mention I am getting married….yup known him for roughly six weeks. Uh-huh? Uh-huh? No, let's talk about this more once you've had a cup of tea and a nice little breather. Oh something's burning, better go. Bye mum, bye!"

Funny she says something is burning, we have nothing cooking as I was going to take her out to a nice little Singaporean restaurant a few blocks down and introduce her to a bit of the stuff my Mam used to make for us.

Zasha comes over grimacing, "My mum is coming, and she wants to meet you."

The frenzied fear in her eyes makes me gulp. I hope Zasha isn't having second thoughts about our impending nuptials.

Fuck. Why can't anything be simple?

The End

(unless you're morbidly curious about what happened to the clamps. In which case *cough*…. keep turning dem pages.)

~~SMUTASTIC~~ EXTRA EPILOGUE: JINGLE BELLS, JIGGLING ALL THE WAY

Author Note: If you hold Jingle Bells sacred, you may want to steer clear of this chapter. It's for anyone who is dearly curious about the clamps Jai had under the Christmas tree for Zasha. Enough said.

Zasha

~One week before Christmas~

"I mean, I would have preferred earrings," I say, as I behold the festive nipple clamps with green bows and bells at the end.

Having just had a shower I have one fluffy white towel wrapped around my body and another around my hair. Jai is wearing his Christmassy peppermint-stripe boxers and nothing else, his hard lean torso on full appetising display. He is sitting on the edge of the bed, just staring. When he looks at me like that I can feel the heat rise and arousal pool between my thighs.

"Hey, maybe I can wear these for when Mum visits," I joke – holding the nipple clamps to my ears.

Jai growls, and picking up the reindeer ears we wore when we ran amok in London he approaches me as I pretend to wear the nipple clamps for earrings.

Jai stands behind me, his chest flush to my back, stirring a frisson of anticipation. He runs a hand down my shoulder before he untwists the towel on my head. My hair is somewhat moulded in the shape of the towel which makes him smile, using my fingers I tug my hair out into a big foxy afro. Jai loves my hair when it is fluffed out into an afro…he likes to stick his fingers in, amazed by how stretchy my hair is. I don't let him near it unless we're making love.

Jai places the reindeer ears headband firmly onto my afro and kisses my forehead, "I love your hair. It's so sexy, just like you Zasha…and with this headband…well *hello* Rudolph," with that remark he slaps my bottom in earthy appreciation.

"Oww!" I cry out as he massages my bottom to soothe it, like the delicious bastard that he is.

"Give me the clamps. You'll like them," Jai gruffly demands. I bet he had a merry old time shopping for these off the internet.

I turn around to face him, "If I'll like these so much then maybe we should start with you," I suggest while clutching my towel protectively around me. I mean, has he ever used these things before, on anyone?

He shrugs, "Okay. I'm good with that."

Smiling evilly I arch a brow as I present the clamps. Levelling each clamp with his little nipples I screw them on. They weigh his tiny nipples down and I can see his eyes doing something squinty.

"Lovely," he says hoarsely. Yeah nope, he's not loving them at all.

"If that's so lovely, give them a shake."

His eyes narrow and he shakes them, "Ah…ah…ah!" he exclaims painfully, the skin around his nipples now looking sore and red as he jingles the bells.

"Still lovely?" I taunt. God, I am a terrible person.

He nods while his face suggests he's swallowed bitter lemons.

Sighing I pat his reddened chest, "No Jai, you're hating it. Absolutely hating it."

I turn around and remove the clamps, but as I stop clutching my towel to attend to the clamps, it drops. Despite his agony, Jai smiles cheekily at my naked form.

Jai uses the opportunity to slip the clamps out of my clutches, "My turn."

"You haven't exactly sold me on them," could I be more sceptical? Nope.

With a hand on my shoulder he guides me to face the mirror, "You'll love 'em."

"Like you just loved them? Hmm, nope. If I hate them, you better take them off," I grumble.

Standing behind me he kisses my neck gently and then with a sadistic expression snakes his hands forward while he watches me in the mirror. With great diligence, he screws the clamp delicately onto my nipple. The sensation isn't bad at all, in fact it's a pleasurable sensation of *good* hurt. The sort of hurt that makes you ache for more. Every little movement causes the festive bell at the end of the clamps to jingle, while the oscillations ring through like a shuddering zip of electricity to my core.

He then whispers into my ear, "But for this last clamp, I'm going to need to go a little lower."

"What are you going to do Jai? Doesn't the last one just go on the other nipple?" mildly concerned I purse my lips together.

"You'll see," he then moves in front of me and drops down to his knees, so that he is level with my sex.

Jai manoeuvres in front of me, propping my leg over his broad shoulder. Nearly losing my balance one hand snakes into Jai's floppy hair to steady myself.

He then starts to tighten the nipple clamp onto my clit, the cool metal causing me to jerk in surprise. As the clamp squeezes around the hood of my nub an extremely delicious sensation licks me down there. I let out a gasp, Jai chuckles in satisfaction - his breath against my cunt- as he does so.

Stroking my fingers through his floppy hair I wonder how my depraved fiancé comes up with this stuff, "God, where do you get these ideas from Jai?"

"Fantasizing about you," he looks up at me with an expression of near reverence before he smiles almost bashfully.

But that mischievous feral grin comes back. Then he gently flicks the bells attached to the clamp on my nub and the vibrations zap up my core, accompanied by the obscene ringing of a tiny bell.

"Oh my gosh," I groan, my fingers tightening around his hair, my body shaking; the bells jingle even more.

"Now Zasha, my turn. Shake them for me, come on, I did it for you," Jai says huskily. Jai grabs my hips and shakes them side to side, causing me to jingle, sending reverberations and a delicious ache to course up from my honeyed core to the nape of my neck.

"Jingle bells, jingle all the way…come on, perhaps you need help to jingle, like this," Jai says roughly, and then dips his face between my thighs, his long tongue lapping at the clamp at my nub, rendering me hot and wet as he licks between the lips of my sex. His hands grasp my thighs needily as if the taste of my pleasure is his nectar.

Shaking as he pleasures me, the obscene jingling only gets louder; my nipple and nub feel aflame with a delicious burning sensation. I peek at myself in the mirror, panting away with reindeer ears and little tinkling bells. Jai between my legs, gripping my thighs. Seeing the broad 'V' of his back flex in the mirror reflection is the tipping point, and soon I feel the familiar roll that grips my body in its ecstasy, as Jai flicks his tongue on my swollen, tormented nub.

"Oh my gosh," I cry out, throwing my head back. Then Jai tugs off the clamp on my clit. The pulsing surge thrums within me and I double over, my hands gripping Jai's shoulders as I coat his handsome face in my arousal. I flutter within, my body jerking from the strength of the climax.

"Jesus Zasha, I need to be buried within you. I want to feel how soaked you are," Jai groans.

Jai arises and looms over me. He wraps his arms around my waist in a hug, pulling me against his erection, "Can you feel how hard I am for you? Are you going to do something about that?" he purrs.

Licking my lips I stare at him probably quite sluttily. Pushing him down onto the bed until he is flat on his back I straddle him.

The nipple clamp is beginning to pinch, "The nipple clamp is hurting."

Jai smiles, his eyes sleepy from lust, "Here, let me help you with that."

He tugs it off with his teeth, it jingles merrily as he does so. The release of it sends the blood rushing back to the nipple, making it tingle even more.

"God you're so sexy. On your knees and facing the mirror, I want to watch you as you come again riding me," Jai squeezes my thighs.

I position myself in front of the mirror, with my little reindeer ears and a rouged nipple. Jai climbs behind me and clutches a handful of my afro hair, gently pulling my head back.

"My naughty, delicious fiancé…there aren't enough Christmases for what I want to do with you," he strokes his cock and then roughly works the head in. Taking full advantage of my wetness he grips my hips and pounds me until I am practically seeing stars.

"Oh my god Jai, yes…harder," thrusting backwards to meet his cock my breasts bounce as I feel another descent into a tightening bliss, coiling round my core.

"Look at yourself, delicious girl," Jai demands gruffly, and forces me to watch in the mirror as he rides me, gripping my hair. In the reflection my gaze travel up to meet his and with this eye contact I clamp around his engorged cock and feel the orgasm tug at every part of me, tug at him inside of me, not wanting to let him go.

"God yes Zasha, take me in, all of it," Jai thrusts hard, grabbing my hair to force me back onto his shaft before his seed coats me from the inside, coming hard and deep.

We both breathe hard, and then he picks me up and sitting on the edge of the bed with his legs spread places me between his legs. The bedding beneath me develops a wet patch from my wetness. He wraps his arms around me.

"I love you Zasha, Merry Christmas," He says as he nibbles my earlobe.

"Merry Christmas my baddie elf," Kissing him on the lips I smile. This must be my favourite version of Jingle Bells yet.

The End

(Really.)

THANK YOU FOR READING.

If you are interested in hearing more from this author then please sign up for the Izzy Coco newsletter:

The Izzy Coco Newsletter

Also, if you could take the time to review or rate this book, that would be gorgeous xxxxx

If you would like to send me feedback directly my email address is:-

izzycocoreads@gmail.com

Printed in Great Britain
by Amazon